REBOUND

BY KWAME ALEXANDER

ILLUSTRATIONS BY
DAWUD ANYABWILE

Clarion Books
An Imprint of HarperCollins*Publishers*
Boston   New York

For Mommy

Clarion Books
An Imprint of HarperCollins Publishers, registered in the United States of America and/or other jurisdictions.

www.clarionbooks.com

The text was set in Adobe Garamond Pro.
Book design by Lisa Vega and Sammy Yuen

The Library of Congress has cataloged the hardcover edition as follows:
Names: Alexander, Kwame, author. | Anyabwile, Dawud, 1965– illustrator.
Title: Rebound / by Kwame Alexander ; illustrations by Dawud Anyabwile.
Description: Boston : HarperCollins, [2018] | Prequel to: The crossover. | Summary: In the summer of 1988, twelve-year-old Chuck Bell is sent to stay with his grandparents, where he discovers jazz and basketball and learns more about his family's past.
Identifiers: LCCN 2018006630 (print) | LCCN 2017061480 (ebook)
Subjects: | CYAC: Novels in verse. | Basketball—Fiction. | Families—Fiction. | African Americans—Fiction. | Washington (D.C.)—History—20th century—Fiction. | BISAC: JUVENILE FICTION / Family / Multigenerational.| JUVENILE FICTION / Sports & Recreation / General. | JUVENILE FICTION / People & Places / United States / African American. | JUVENILE FICTION / Historical / United States / 20th Century. | JUVENILE FICTION / Boys & Men.
Classification: LCC PZ7.5.A44 (print) | LCC PZ7.5.A44 Re 2018 (ebook) | DDC [Fic]—dc23
LC record available at https://lccn.loc.gov/2018006630

ISBN: 978-0-544-86813-7 hardcover
ISBN: 978-0-358-49483-6 paperback

Manufactured in the United States of America
22 23 24 25 26 LBC 10 9 8 7 6

Looking Back

It was the summer
when Now and Laters

cost a nickel
and *The Fantastic Four,*

a buck.
When I met

Harriet Tubman
and the Harlem Globetrotters.

It was the hottest summer
after the coldest winter ever,

when a storm shattered
my home

into a million little pieces
and soaring above

the sorrow and grief
seemed impossible.

It was the summer of 1988,
when basketball gave me wings

and I had to learn
how to rebound

on the court.
And off.

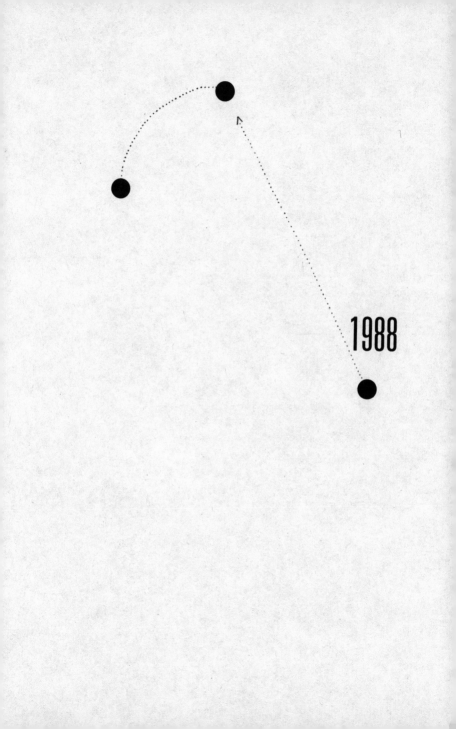

1988

May 28, 1988

The game is on
at the park.
The stars are out.
It's close to dark.
Hoop Kings
SOARing
      in the *SKY*
      so high
      so fly
like they Got Wings
(it's like the blacktop
is a box**SPRING**)
Hey, Charlie, you see what he did with that THING!
my best friend, Skinny, yells
T
   W
     I
      R
        L
          I
            N
               G and *WHIRLING* the ball

so sweet

it's like a bee s t i n g

(Ouch!)

He just Swished

in your *Face.*

Stung you like

a can of *mace*

These boys so fly

they're outta ***SPACE!***

C'mon, Charlie, I got next. Let's hoop, Skinny says,

jumping up from the sidewalk.

Nah, I gotta get home for dinner, I lie.

I used to play H.O.R.S.E.

against my father, and sometimes I
won, but when I tried playing on
a team, I'd get too nervous
to shoot, too scared of the
ball (like the time I
missed a pass and
got hit up-
side the
head).

7

Sometimes, I wish

I was a superhero,
superfly
like Quicksilver
speed-racing
down the court
sleek as a sports car
faster than NASCAR,
leaving all my sadness
in the dust—far,
far away
from now.

Wish I could soar
score
throw down
a monster dunk
like I was Thor.

Wish I could elevate
my name
with game so good
it's hall of fame!

8

Wish I could forget
all the pain.

Yeah, that's what I wish . . .

Skinny picks

some other boy
to be on his team,

which is cool with me,
'cause I'd much rather be

at home
lying across

my bed
reading comics.

See you tomorrow, Skinny,
I yell,

but he's already
on the court

running a game
and his mouth.

12

Home

The Fantastic Four
chase
Galactus
through the universe
on a time sled
when they get sucked into
a black hole
that nearly burns them
to *holy hand grenades*.

But Thor's hammer
KABOOMS them
outta impending doom,
right smack in the middle
of an intergalactic civil war
between armed battleships
that makes *Star Wars*
look like a playground fight.

Before they get shot up,
Reed
a.k.a. Stretch
a.k.a. Mister Fantastic

uses THE TIME DILATION EFFECT
to freeze EVERYTHING
and move them back
in time.

I wish
I could do
the same thing
and get outta
this black hole
I'm trapped in . . .

14

Black Hole

My dad was a star
in our neighborhood.
Everybody knew him.

He taught
adults to read
in the mornings,

and taught
night school
to kids

with problems
who got kicked
out of regular school.

Each summer
just me and him
would pack up

his pickup truck
and road trip
to as many state capitals

as we could
in the two weeks
he had for vacation.

My least favorite
was Dover, Delaware,
'cause the major tourist attraction

was a mortuary
that processed
the remains

of over 50,000 soldiers.
This year,
I turned twelve

and he promised
to take me
to the Appalachians,

Charleston,
Knoxville,
Louisville,

to hike,
and he promised
to get me

some fresh sneakers
and let me
taste beer,

as long as
*You don't tell
your mother, Charlie.*

But none of that ever happened
because at 9:01 p.m.
on the ninth of March

my star exploded
and everything
froze.

Conversation

Why aren't you doing your homework?
Mom, can't you knock first.

It's my house, I don't have to knock. I asked you a question.
It's the end of school, we don't really have homework.

Can you put your comic book down for a second? I want to talk with you.
What?

Don't say WHAT *to me.*
Yes?

Summer's here in two weeks, and I was thinking maybe we could go to Boston or Providence.
Why?

They're capitals.
No thanks.

C'mon, Charlie, it'll be fun.
I don't want to go there.

Then how about SeaWorld?
No thanks.

Honey, you loved SeaWorld.
Yeah, and I also sat in a car seat when I was four, but
you know things change, Mom.

Charlie Bell, always a comedian.
. . .

There's an overnight basketball camp.
I don't like basketball.

Since when?
Since now. Plus, I don't have any sneakers.

Then what are those things I bought you for Christmas.
Nobody wears *Zips*, Mom.

They make your feet run faster, she says, giggling.
Be serious, Mom. I hate those sneakers.

*Be grateful for what you have, Charlie. Some kids don't
even have shoes to wear.*
. . .

How were your tests?
Fine.

. . .

Can I have some money for lunch?

I gave you lunch money on Monday.
It's gone.

Lunch money is for lunch, not comics.
Well, pay me allowance like all my friends get.

Allowance? How about I allow you to have clothes and food and shelter?
So we're just always gonna be poor?

We have everything we need.
Not everything.

20 . . .

. . .

Charlie, just tell me what you want to do.
I want. To read. My comics. Okay!

That's all you've been doing lately. I miss you.
What are you talking about? I'm right here.

Let's play Scrabble or cards, then.
Stop acting like everything's normal. IT'S NOT!

Then let's talk about what happened.

. . .

I know you're sad, but—
I'M MAD!

That's why we have to talk about it.
I don't have nothing to say.

Anything. I don't have anything to say.
Whatever, I mumble.

Look, you can be angry, but you can't be disrespectful.
. . .

We'll finish this later. Dinner's ready, come on downstairs.
I don't want noth— anything to eat.   21

In the Morning

Each day I wake to the BOOM BAP of
my clock radio playing rap
music, but today I'm blasted
by a loud siren that
jolts me awake and
sends me back to
that day when
my life
changed.

Ten Reasons Why I Hate Sirens

Because I hadn't eaten dinner and I was starving
Because he was making me a grilled cheese
Because I told him a joke and he screamed with laughter
Because the laughing stopped, but the screaming didn't
Because I heard him drop the pan on the floor
Because he said his chest hurt and he dropped to
    the floor
Because his eyes were rolling like pinballs
Because I dialed 9-1-1 but kept pressing the
    wrong numbers
Because she said the ambulance was on the way
Because *on the way* felt like light-years.

Today

I miss the bus
to school
because I can't find
my library books,
which are due,
which I thought
were on my desk,
but it turns out
are under
my dirty clothes,
which are under
a blanket
under my bed.

Somewhere between
eating a strawberry Pop-Tart
and not calling Mom
at work
to let her know
I missed the bus,
I decide
to just skip
school,

which means
I won't have
to listen
to my other best friend, CJ,
go on and on
about artificial snow
or whatever
wacky experiment
she's into now, and
I won't have
to listen to Skinny
sing
Michael Jackson songs
and argue
with me
over who's the best
baller
of all time:

Him: Dr. J
Me: Kareem Abdul-Jabbar

Today,
I skip school
for the first time ever
so I won't have to listen,

so I won't have to laugh,
so I won't have to pretend
like the center
of my universe
didn't collapse.

There's an old house

on my block
that we never see
anyone coming out of
or going into.

Sometimes
there are empty
soda bottles
next to a rocking chair
on the porch
that no one ever sits in,
but in the mornings,
on the bus,
we can see
the chair
rocking.

Word is,
Old Lady Wilson
lives there
with fourteen cats
and her dead husband
and sits on a
plastic-covered sofa
with a shotgun

and no teeth,
chewing tobacco
and waiting for us,
daring us
to step one foot
on her property
or commit a crime
(like throw trash
in her yard
or play hooky
from school)
so she can torture
and torment us.

I don't know
if I believe it,
but while I'm walking
past her house
on my way
to playing hooky,
I swear I see
her curtains move,
and since I don't want
to risk my life,
I run.

Fast.

Sanctuary

About a twenty-minute walk
from my house
is an old shopping center
with a new grocery store,
pizza restaurant,
Family Dollar,
and a smelly arcade
called Flipper McGhees
where me and Dad
used to battle
each other
in Pac-Man.

Flipper McGhees

After six tries
I finally make it
to level three,
about to nail
the high score,
when I hear
Skinny's voice
and feel a hard tug
on my arm.

CHARLIE. THE COPS ARE HERE!

Then, I hear an unfamiliar voice:
Hey, you! KID, COME BACK HERE!

If you get caught
skipping school,
the truant officers
put you in jail
overnight
with bread and water
and a pot
to pee in,

so when Skinny yells,
RUN,
I do.
Fast.

Me and Skinny

have been friends
since we met
at CJ's tenth birthday
roller-skating party,
where we raced
each other,
joked each other,
and started our own
Friday-night skate crew
called

the Three Amigos,
but then CJ said
we had to change
the name
because she was
an amig-A,
not an amig-O.

Skinny's good at skating,
not so good
at basketball
(even though he swears
he's a baller),
and even worse
at remembering stuff,

like the combination
to his locker
(good thing me and CJ know it)
or the keys
to his house,
which he can never find
after school.

He and his mom
stay at
his aunt
and uncle's house
in the basement
'cause his father got
shell-shocked
in Vietnam
and now walks around
their old neighborhood
mumbling
to himself
about Mars,
whiskey,
and Hamburger Hill.

Conversation with Skinny

You skipping school?
Yeah.

Why didn't you tell me?
Why didn't you tell me?

. . .

. . .

That was close, man.
Yep.

They caught one dude.
Dag.

You like my kicks?
Yeah, but they're too big for you? You almost tripped
back there.

They're my cousin's.
He let you wear his Jordans?

Nope, but what he doesn't know won't hurt him.
They're fresh.

Fresh to death.
My mom's buying me some too.

No more ZZZZZZZZZips, he says, laughing. *About time,*
Charlie.
Yeah, I say, lying again, knowing she's told me no
twice already, *I'm not spending a hundred dollars*
on a pair of sneakers, Charlie!

Me too, Charlie. We're both gonna be like Jordan.
Yep.

Thought

Why can't
my mother
understand
that the shoes
are not just
for my feet
but my heart,
too?

Who's Bad?

I bet you I could dunk in these sneakers.
Doubt it.

Jordan did. Remember him in the dunk contest?
Yeah.

He was wearing these right here, Skinny says, pointing to
his cousin's (borrowed) sneakers.

...

You like my new jacket?
It's a jacket.

*It's a Michael Jackson jacket. My granny sent it for my
birthday.*
Your birthday was in January.

She doesn't shop when it's cold out.
I guess that means she's cold-blooded.

Yo, that's funny. Hey, Charlie, who's bad?
You, Skinny, I say, shaking my head.

You know it! Ready for the skating contest?
Yeah, I guess.

'Cause the summer's here, and it's time to par-tay. CJ's dad's taking us. He is soooo cool!

. . .

Oh—sorry, man. I didn't mean to bring that up.

. . .

I heard you had to get a job.
No! Why would I—

Because, you know, what happened, you know—
That's stupid. My mom has enough money.

Yeah, I thought so . . . Hey, can I come over to your house tonight?
For dinner?

Nah, to watch MTV. They're showing DJ Jazzy Jeff & the Fresh Prince's music video.
Why can't you watch it at your place?

'Cause my mom cuts off the TV and makes me read.
A book?

Yeah.
Is it a good one?

Is any book good?
True. You can borrow one of my comics.

I wish. She doesn't like comics.
But you're the one reading.

Sometimes she wants us to read together. It sucks.
Yeah, that does.

So, can I come over?
I don't know. My mom trips out too much.

. . .

. . .

AW, MAN!
What?

I think I left my dollar bill, he says, still checking his pockets.
Where?

On the pinball machine.
What was your dollar bill doing on the pinball machine?

I was about to get some coins when the cops came in.
. . .

That was my allowance for the rest of the week.

I guess you're not a smooth criminal, Skinny, I say, smiling.

Not funny, bro!

Hooky

His house
is empty
and full of
cigarette stink.

My uncle smokes incessantly.
Huh?

It means nonstop. CJ kept saying I was talking incessantly,
so I looked it up.
Oh.

Skinny plays
video games.

We eat
watermelon
Now and Laters.

I reread
The Fantastic Four
beginning with #1,

and try
not to cry
for the eightieth day
in a row.

Memory

I beat
Mom home
go to my room
shut my door
and stare
at the picture
of Dad
in front of
the *Welcome to Georgia* sign.

When she knocks
I pull out
my notebook
and pretend
to do homework.

Hey there, Charlie. Tell me about your day at school . . .

I skipped school today

and drank soda
and didn't eat lunch
and I almost got arrested
and I hate math
and tomorrow we have to play basketball in gym class
and I'm not that good
and I'm not that good at anything
and who's gonna teach me everything?
and do I need to get a job?
and why is everybody always sorry?
and CJ's dad is soooo cool
and I'm not taking a shower tonight
because I didn't do anything all day
but read comics
and play Pac-Man
and I still don't feel
any better
than I did
last week
or yesterday
or when I woke up
and I'm tired
so can I please
just stay
in my room

turn out the lights
and hide
inside the darkness
that owns me?
Please.

Charlie, I asked you how was school?

After dinner

I turn on MTV
to watch
the music video

for "Parents Just Don't Understand,"
which is hot
and funny

and the motto
of my life,
but I don't get

to finish it,
because someone
cuts the TV off.

OOPS!

MOM, WHY'D YOU—
I told you I don't want you watching inappropriate
television.

It's just a video, I say, and turn it back on.
CHARLES, TURN. OFF. THE. TV.

Her nostril flares up
her left eyebrow lifts—the look
when she's about to trip out—so I
turn it off.
Fast.

It's not fair. You can't just do that.
It's my house and I can absolutely do that. I'm concerned
about you.

She tries to hold my hand.
I pull away.

I didn't want to watch the stupid TV, anyway.
But—

But, nothin'. I'm outta here, I say, running down the hall,
slamming my bedroom door—

OOPS—
in her face.

Conversation (that ends badly)

HAVE YOU LOST YOUR MIND?
. . .

I'M TALKING TO YOU!
Just leave me alone.

LEAVE YOU ALONE?! Boy, I am this close to wringing your neck.
And, I'll call Child Protective Services, I mumble, just loud enough for her not to hear me.

What did you say! WHAT DID YOU SAY!
I'm sick of this place. I'm sick of everything.

Get used to it, 'cause you're gonna be even sicker. You're grounded until further notice. Go to school, come home, no TV, no video games.
That's just stupid. Dad would never do that.

. . .

I wish he was here and you weren't.

. . .

. . .

You know what, you think you mean that . . . That's a cruel thing to say, Charlie.

. . .

Put that comic book away, cut off these lights, and go to bed. NOW!
WHAT?! So now I can't even read. You're punishing my brain.

I don't want to hear another word from you. Go to bed. I'm done. No bath, just wash your face and go to bed.

. . .

50 *DID. YOU. HEAR. ME?*
Yes.

Then move. ***NOW!***

. . .

Overheard

I don't know how to reach him. I know he's in pain, but—

. . .

I know it takes time, I do, but I just don't know what to do.

. . .

He's got so much anger inside, and then I get mad, and we can't just keep going like this.

. . .

I guess he's doing okay. He doesn't talk to me about school.

. . .

School's out in three days, and I really can't afford it, but I thought we'd go on a vacation, just the two—

. . .

Yes, I thought about a psychiatrist, or some sort of camp, but I can't afford—

. . .

I appreciate that. Anything's got to be better than this,
'cause I can't handle him. I swear, I'm not going to be able
to keep this together.

. . .

I'll think about that, thank you.

. . .

Things I Think About Before I Fall Asleep

What is she thinking about?
Who was she talking to on the phone?
Why can't I get a real pair of sneakers?
What am I going to do this summer?
Will I have to get a job?
Where is my father now?

Lunch

What's she doing with the magnet? Skinny asks, pointing
to CJ, who's sitting across the lunch table from us.
Cereal is "fortified with iron," CJ answers, conducting an
experiment on her cereal.

Forty-five with iron? What's that?
Fortified, Skinny. To strengthen, as in—

AS IN, he interrupts, flexing his biceps, *look at these
fortified guns I got, right?*
*Seriously, haven't y'all ever wondered why cereal says
"fortified with iron"?*

I didn't know cereal could talk, Skinny says, laughing at
his corny joke.
Nah, not really, I say to CJ.

*Our bodies need iron to carry oxygen to fix our blood. So
where does it come from?*
Not from the cereal, stupid, Skinny says, still laughing.

You're stupid, Skinny. Plus, I'm done. There's no metal in here.
You really thought there was metal in there, CJ? I ask.

*Of course not, Charlie, but science is about proof. Now I
know for sure.*
Oh.

Hey, where were you guys yesterday?
Me and Charlie cut yesterday, Skinny says, winking at me
with a mouthful of Tater Tots.

Y'all skipped school without me?
Sorry, CJ, I say.

It's not like you would've come with us, Skinny says.
True, but a girl likes to be asked.

*I can't wait for gym today. We're playing ball, and I'm
showing up and showing off.*
You're always showing off, Skinny. You're a ball hog.

Am not.
Charlie, what's the difference between Skinny and time?
she asks.

I don't know, CJ, I say.
Time passes, she says, and

I laugh
so hard,
I almost spit out
my chocolate milk.

In preschool

CJ would
knock down
my ABC blocks
then take them
and spell
words
nobody recognized,
sometimes not even
the teachers.

One day
she spelled
FRIENDS,
then pointed
at me.

We've been
tight as twins
ever since.

Things I Think About in Gym Class

Why don't they have air conditioning in our gym?
Why does Skinny pull his socks way up past his knees?
CJ jokes on Skinny a lot.
My dad said that when a girl picks on you, it means she
    likes you.
I hope Mr. Johnson doesn't call on me to play in this
    stupid game.

Unlucky

Mr. Johnson
picks me
to play

in the first game.
The ball feels
heavy

and strange
in my hands.
I stand there

dribbling,
listening
to my name

being called
over and over:
CHARLIE, PASS THE BALL!

I stand there
wishing.
Wishing

I was . . .

Lucky

Midgame,
the fire alarm
goes off.

I drop
the ball
and we quickly

line up
to exit
the gym.

Chills

We haven't had a drill since before
Christmas, so when the fire trucks
arrive with their ghostly
sirens, I start sweating,
shaking, and feeling
sick in my gut
like it's the
ninth of
March.

Yo, Charlie, you all right?

Everything blurs.

My ears ring
with the sound
of sirens
and Skinny screaming,
HIT 'IM ON THE BACK!
and CJ screaming back,
HE'S NOT CHOKING, STUPID!

I feel my face boil
and then a geyser
of peanut butter
and chocolate milk
shoots out
all over
the sidewalk
in front of
my whole class.

Use your magnet on that, CJ, Skinny says,
which kinda makes me laugh,
even though
I really wanna cry.

Queasy

Thanks for coming with me to the nurse, guys.
We're the Three Amigos, that's how we roll, Skinny says.

The Two Amigos plus one Amiga, CJ corrects.
I feel a little better now.

*It was probably the chocolate milk that messed up your
stomach. It tasted like it had a fizz.*
It wasn't the milk, CJ says.

You don't know that, CJ.

*The brain and the stomach are tightly linked. Studies have
shown not only that the mind has an effect on the gut,
but—*

Speak English, girl, Skinny says.
*When you get real nervous, your brain sends a signal to the
stomach. He's probably still thinking about what happened.
Aren't you, Charlie?*

. . .

CJ, for somebody with book sense, you don't have any common sense. We're not supposed to talk about that, remember?

Sorry, Charlie.
. . .

After School

The note
on the refrigerator
that reads
Had to work a second shift
at the hospital. Finish your homework.
Dinner's in the oven. Put your dishes away,
then call your grandmother
and say happy birthday. And
don't forget to put the trash out.
Love, Mom
is like an invitation
to fun
and freedom.
I mean, I know
she didn't say
I could go
outside and play,
but she didn't say
I couldn't either,
plus we finished
our tests last week,
and, with two days left,
the teachers don't

really give
homework
anymore.

After not eating

the meat loaf
and baked potato
and broccoli,
I call Skinny
but he's at the court,
so I ring CJ
to see
if she wants
to play video games
or walk the block
(or study, I guess)
but *She's not home,*
her dad reminds me:
She's on an overnight trip
to Columbia University
in New York
to be interviewed
for junior inventors camp.

So I read.

An hour later,
my doorbell rings.

Nine times.

Conversation (at my front door)

Heard you were looking for me.
Just seeing if you wanted to hang out.

We were at the court.
Y'all win?

We didn't finish. We were losing, then Ivan got in a fight,
he says, pointing to the end of my driveway, where his
older cousin, Ivan, stands.
Oh.

Come on, Skinny, or I'm leaving you! Ivan hollers from
the street.
*Hey, Charlie, me and Ivan are going to the store. C'mon,
go with us.*

Nah, I gotta stay home.
We can get some Now or Laters.

I used all my money on comics.
I got you.

Maybe, but we gotta be quick. My mom gets home
soon.

Hey, Charlie, can you run in those busted sneakers?
Ivan hollers.

Huh? Yeah, I can run, I say to him, grabbing my key
and shutting the front door.
Just come on then, punk, he says, grinding his teeth like
a pit bull.

Ivan

used to be
pretty cool
and fun
to be around
till he started
smoking
and hanging out
with a group
of delinquents
he met
in juvie.

On our way to Quik-Mart

Ivan the Terrible stops
at the fence
behind
Old Lady Wilson's.

Why are we stopping? I say. She could be watching us.
She's asleep, punk.

Ivan shares
his theory
that old people
take naps at five o'clock
every day
right before dinner,
so they
can stay up late
and watch
The Johnny Carson Show.

That's stupid.
*He's right, Charlie. My grandparents nap. The old guy next
door to us naps.*

I been casing this joint for weeks, y'all, Ivan says.
He's been watching too much TV, I say to Skinny,
who nods.

*I got a plan. Y'all know those bottles she keeps in those boxes
on her porch?*
Yeah, Skinny says.

Once a month, some guy comes and picks up the boxes, Ivan
continues.
Yeah, so?

*Last month he didn't come, so there's two months' worth of
boxes out there.*
And?

The Quik-Mart pays ten cents a bottle.
SO YOU WANNA STEAL HER SODA BOTTLES?

Shhhhh! You're gonna blow our cover.
I'm not stealing nothin'. Especially from Old Lady
Wilson. She's got a shotgun.

*That's a rumor. Plus, she's asleep. Now come on
let's do this,* Skinny says.
I'm not stealing those bottles.

Charlie, stop being a wimp. She's not gonna miss those
bottles. The guy probably doesn't even bring her back
the money. We can get some Funyuns and a Slurpee.
Good luck, I'm outta—

But, before I can say

no again,
Ivan says,
Come on, Skinny,
and takes off
like a ninja
with Skinny
right behind him.

They grab
the boxes,
run back
toward me
yelling
RUN! RUN, CHARLIE!

So I run,
and don't stop
until
we get to
the Quik-Mart.

The Loot

We cash in
sixty-two bottles,
then I head home
with my loot,
making sure
to take
the long way
to avoid
loaded shotguns.

Interruption

I'm almost done
reading about shape-changing
aliens trying
to conquer the earth
when Skinny calls.

Yo, that was kinda fun, he says.
Yeah, for you maybe, I answer.

Whatchu doing?
I can't really talk, Skinny, I say, wanting to get back to
my comic. I'll see you tomorrow, Skinny.

Nope, you won't, he says.
You skipping again?

Nah! Got caught bouncing my ball in the hallway.
In-school suspension.
Dag.

I drift off

finishing
issue #2,
where the Skrulls
impersonate
the Fantastic Four
and wonder
if that's what's happening
to me,
'cause I just don't feel
like myself.

Alarm

Instead of
the sound
of music
I wake to
the sound
of my mom
growling
and staring
at me
with the eyes
of a tiger.

WAKE UP, CHARLIE!
Huh?

She cuts
the lights on.
It's like a super laser beam
aimed right at me.

WAKE UP, I hear her screaming.
Wha— what's going on?

What's this? she asks, holding up an empty bag of
Funyuns.
What's what, Mom?

I found this in the trash.
The trash? Can you cut those blinding lights off, please?

GET. UP! she screams again, this time pulling the covers
off me.
MOM, it's like four-thirty. In the morning.

*IF YOU WANT TO MAKE IT TO 4:31, YOU BETTER
TELL ME WHAT THIS IS!*

. . .

Interrogation

I'm waiting.
It was just Funyuns, I say, wishing I had remembered to
put out the trash.

*It wasn't JUST Funyuns. I made your favorite meat loaf,
but I come home to find dinner still in the oven, two dozen
candy wrappers and this junk food in the trash can that I
know I asked you to put out. I know this, because it's on the
note I found in the trash can.*

. . .

Where'd you get the money from?
Money for what?

For the dinner you got from Quik-Mart.
Huh?

Charlie, don't mess with me. I asked you a question.
I had it left over from lunch.

*That's a lie. You just asked me for lunch money two days
ago, remember? You took lunch, so what's the deal, Charlie?*

Tell me the truth, or else.

Or else what? I say, wondering how that slipped out.

And wishing it hadn't.

Trouble

I remember
my father spanking me
when I was little,
but the most
my mother ever did
was raise her voice.
Until now.

Her hand
is like
a razor-sharp claw
about to slice
the air
lightning fast
in the direction
of my face,
but I duck
before the blast
almost rips
my head off.

The Truth

OKAY, OKAY, Mom, I say, frantically. I kinda
borrowed some
Coke bottles
from Mrs. Wilson
and returned them
to the store
and used the refund
to buy snacks
and I'm sorry,
REALLY, REALLY, SORRY,
Mom,
and I'll never
do that again
is what I say.

Put on your clothes and come downstairs is what
she says, real soft-like,
then walks out.

Dead Man Walking

I put on my shorts
and hoodie,
prepared to
mop the kitchen floor,
clean the garage,
or whatever punishment chore
she's figured
will make me a better person
and whatnot,
but when I get downstairs

she's got on her jacket
with a purse
on her arm
and the front door is open
and she's standing
on the other side
of it,
looking as mean
as a prison dog,
like she's about to
escort me
to death row.

The sky looks

silvery blue
and lifeless
at FIVE A.M.
and just when
I get up the nerve
to ask her
why we're walking
beneath it—about
twenty steps
from my house—I
find out.
I. Find. Out.

THIS. CAN'T. BE. HAPPENING!

She makes me knock

and right before
my knuckles hit

the front door
for the third time

it opens
swiftly

my teeth clench
and I pray

there's not a witch
or a warlock

or a woman
with a shotgun

on the other side
of the door.

A very big dog

marches toward me,
head down,

and I move, fast.
Hide behind

my mom.
He almost knocks

us both over, then
sniffs us,

till wicked Old Lady Wilson
calls him back.

She doesn't look so scary
in her pink housecoat

lopsided wig
and the false teeth

she fumbles with
before putting them in her mouth,

smiling as wide as the sea,
and saying *Come on in, Charlie Bell*

like she's been waiting
for me.

Mrs. Wilson, we're not going to stay, my mom says. *Like I
said on the phone, my son has something he'd like to say to you.*
I do?

Thought

Her house
smells
like a cross
between grass
when it's just cut
and Skinny
after gym class.

Musty.

Great Dane

Her dog is
a zebra—painted white
with black patches—
and HUGE.

She rubs him,
tells him
to sit, and
he's about to
when
the whistling teapot
startles him,
and he interrupts
my *Sorry for stealing your bottles* apology
with a loud
chattering sound
coming from
his mouth.

Her teeth do that when she gets scared or excited, says
Old Lady Wilson as she
rubs him, and—

Wait, did she just say *She?*

Consequence (Part One)

Hush now, girl, before you wake up the neighbors,
Old Lady Wilson says, giving her a snack from her
robe pocket.
So yeah, I'm sorry Mrs.—

Now just hush yourself, Charlie Bell. Those bottles don't
mean nothing to me. My son collects them.

I look at Mom,
wondering
if she's gonna correct
Old Lady Wilson's grammar.
She doesn't.

I will pay you back, I promise.
Nonsense. Keep your money, Charlie Bell. But I could use
some help around here.

Anything you want, Mrs. Wilson, Mom says. *Just name it.*
Well, could he walk Woodrow here?

WHAT!?
He'll be happy to walk her, Mrs. Wilson.

Anytime is fine by me, long as it's not in the early evening.
That's when I take my naps.

Things I Think About on the Walk Home

She named her girl dog Woodrow Wilson?
I wonder if Skinny got in trouble.
Why didn't I put the trash out?
My punishment is walking a dog.
Doesn't Mom know I'm afraid of dogs?
Old Lady Wilson is not as mean as I thought.
Tomorrow's the last day of school.
Tomorrow is the first day of summer.
Tomorrow is my first summer without a road trip.

Bomb

The silence is booming.
Mom doesn't say a word
until we get home.

Then
she detonates.

You want to go to jail, Charlie

because that's what happens to people
who steal. You want to get locked up?
But I didn't even do
anything. I was just
there, and I didn't
even have a choice,
and it was
all his
fault.

Blame

Who is he? she asks,
and I want to
bust on Skinny
for getting me
into all this trouble,
but then
she wouldn't let me
hang out with him
all summer.

98

If he got caught
he probably
wouldn't tell
on me,
so I don't.

The Last Straw

She says she's run
out of patience,
thinks I'm headed
down the wrong path,
knows I'm hurting
and maybe I need
the kind of help
she can't give me.

It was just some boy from around the way. I don't even
really know him, I lie.
Well, you need to remember him, 'cause I don't know is not
good enough, Charlie.

What I need is to get far away from here, I say,
but she doesn't understand
that I'm talking
about this place of sadness
I've been living in
since March ninth,
'cause she starts crying,
then goes into
her room

and slams the door
like she's given up
on me.

School

is a dreadful blur
'cause CJ's not here,
Skinny's in detention
for bouncing his ball
in school,
and I can't stop thinking
about my mess-up
and how
I've never seen
my mom
this mad before.

When I get home

she says hello
without a smile,
then tells me
she's tired
so she's going
to bed early
and that
the suitcases
that were in
our attic
are now on
my bed.

After you eat dinner—it's
in the oven—start packing
all your summer clothes
clean your room
set your alarm
an hour earlier
so you can get up
and walk the dog
before school.
Good night!

Pack for what?

Why I Don't Like Dogs

When I was six, my dad taught me how
to ride a bike and showed me tricks
like bunny-hopping and slides
and one day I tried to
pop a wheelie when
a dog jumped me
and scared me
and I
CRASHED!

Walking Woodrow

I knock
on the door
then back up
down the stairs
of Old Lady Wilson's front porch
in case she (the dog)
comes out
too fast
and too big
and too scary.

She's more afraid of you, Old Lady Wilson says through
her screen door. *Just come on up here and pet her, like this,*
she says, rubbing her head. *C'mon, try it.*
I do, cautiously.

*She's blind as a bat in her left eye, but she can see well
enough to walk, and she needs the exercise. I used to take
her to the park every day before my nap, but that arthritis is
something, I tell ya.*
Oh.

Danes don't like a lot of exercise. Come to think of it, me either, she says, laughing. *So just take her around the block once or twice.*

Once, I mumble to myself.

Unleashed

Woodrow walks
beside me
like we're friends.

We're not.

When we get
to the Millers'
she plays
in their sprinkler
and starts wagging
her tail
in a circular motion
like a propeller.

I almost laugh
until I remember
the last time
I was here.

The Last Day of School

On the bus ride
Skinny listens
to his music,
twirls his ball
on his finger.

CJ can't stop talking
about the pizza
in New York City,
the weird people
in Times Square,
and all the smart students
she met
at Columbia University.

I stare
out the window,
yawning,
wondering why
I have to pack
and hope it's not
for Disney World
or worse
some whack

summer camp
for kids with
grief.

Well, somebody's tired, CJ says, nudging me.
I had to wake up way early, I say.

Why?
To walk Old Lady Wilson's dog.

TO WHAT!?! she and Skinny say in unison.

I tell them

I got in trouble
for doing something
really, REALLY stupid.

I'm sorry, CJ adds.
Yeah, that's messed up, Charlie, Skinny says, clueless.
What'd you do?

Why are you always so nosy? CJ says, rolling her eyes
at him.

Why are you so ring-around-the-rosy, he says, laughing
and high-fiving me, like he just got her good.

Why are you so vexatious? CJ counters.
Huh?

Yeah, that's what I thought, she says, licking her finger
and rubbing the air with it. *Score for CJ!*
I took something that didn't belong to me, I say, and
Skinny's eyes get all big.

That doesn't even sound like you, Charlie Bell.
Was it just you, or did anyone else get in trouble? Skinny
asks, all frantic-like.

I shouldn't have done it, but I owned up to it, and now I gotta walk Old Lady Wilson's dog every morning.
Dang, that kinda sucks. I'd help, but I'm allergic to dogs.

You're allergic to work, Skinny, CJ says. *I can help you, if you want, Charlie.*
Thanks, but her dog is kinda scary.

Dogs are more afraid of us, she says.
Forget about the dog. What I wanna know is, is Old Lady Wilson scary? Skinny asks.

The dog

is white, huge,
bigger than
Old Lady Wilson,
with patches of black,
and she named her
after the twenty-eighth president
of the United States, I say,
but all Skinny wants
to know
is what
Old Lady Wilson looks like
and if it's true
she keeps
her husband's
casket
in the basement.

She named her Abraham Lincoln?

He then asks.
No, stupid, Woodrow Wilson, corrects CJ, who's
probably gonna be
a teacher
when she grows up
'cause her brain
already knows stuff
most adults don't.

Why would she name a girl dog after a guy president?
Skinny asks.
Yeah, I was wondering the same thing.

Probably because he supported the Nineteenth Amendment,
which gave women the right to vote.
Probably not, Skinny says, shaking his head.

Yeah, I doubt that's the reason, I say, but he sounds like
a cool guy.
He also thought slavery and segregation were good things.

Not cool, I say.
Can we not talk about slavery please? It kinda creeps me
out, Skinny says.

How do you know so much stuff, CJ? I ask.

I'm a genius, Charlie. I thought you knew that, she says,

with a smile

and a punch

to my stomach

that hurts

in a good

kind of way.

Sorry you got in trouble. I'll help you walk Woodrow

Wilson, though.

Okay.

Friday

We have parties
in most of our classes
and in the rest,
the teachers
just tell us
to look busy,
so I read comics
while Skinny
talks my head off
about
how he hopes
his mom gets
a better job
so they can move out
and he can get
his own bedroom,
and about
how he thinks
that CJ might like me,
and about how
he's sorry
he got me
in trouble.

It's okay, I tell him.

AW, MAN, he yells, startling the whole class.

What?

I left my ball on the bus this morning.

Saturday

We sit
inches from each other
at the breakfast table
but it feels like
we're in different countries,
our treaty disappearing
with each forkful
of French toast
and each spoonful
of grits,
our distance
growing further
and further
with each
wordless
moment.

The clink
of the knife
slicing bread
is the only sound
between us.
I want to say something
but the words
get in the way.

I take my last bite,
mumble "Thank you,"
get up
to go shower,
then walk
our twenty-eighth president.

Consequence (Part Two)

You're welcome, she says.
I did say thank you.

Anything else you have to say?
. . .

*Because even though you don't want me to be here, I just
made your favorite breakfast, and—*
I didn't really mean what I said.

Well, it sure sounded like you meant it. That was hurtful,
Charlie. And stealing? That's not you.
I'm sorry—I didn't mean to.

Look, it's been a tough time for both of us, and I know you
miss your father. We need a change.
What kind of change?

We need to get away.
I don't want to go to Disney World.

I heard you.
Or camp.

I've got something else in mind.
Like what?

I thought we could visit Grandma and Granddaddy.
Why?

They miss you.
For how long?

I have to work Saturday night, so I would drop you off next Sunday.
NEXT SUNDAY? That's like in a week. And, what do you mean, drop me off?

I want you to spend some time alone with your grandparents.
So you're leaving me there?

It'll be good for both of us.
That's not fair.

I think it would be good for you. And them.
How long do I have to stay there?

The whole summer.
. . .

I almost drop my

plate on the floor when she decides to
ruin my brand-new day with her
cruel and unreasonable
decision to send her
only son away,
but right before
my STORM, the
doorbell
rings.

Three-Way Conversation

Hello, Crystal. What a nice surprise.
What are you doing here, CJ?

Is that the way we talk to guests, Charlie?
It's okay, Mrs. Bell, I'm used to Charlie being cantankerous.
He's dealing with a lot.

Come on in.
How are things at the hospital, Mrs. Bell?

Long hours, but things are good, Crystal.
I might want to be a nurse when I grow up too. Or a
scientist. Or a teacher.

Or a talker, I say, laughing by myself.
Or a dog walker, she comes back with, quickly. *I came*
to help you walk Woodrow Wilson, but maybe I should
reconsider.

. . .

That's very nice of you, Crystal. Well, I'll leave you two to it.
Charlie, come straight back home afterward.

Yeah, okay.
Are you coming to our skating contest on Friday, Mrs. Bell?

I'm afraid Charlie will not be able to participate.
MOM! Why not! That's just not fair.

Charlie, we can discuss this later.
That's a shame, Mrs. Bell. I understand, but it's certainly
disappointing. We've been practicing our routine for
months, and we have a chance to win the finals, and
Skinny's grounded because he got a D in English but his
mother is letting him skate because if one of us doesn't come
we won't be able to compete, and my parents are coming,
and—

Okay, thank you, Crystal. Is this true, Charlie?
Yeah.   123

. . .
I mean, yes.

Well, we will see. Maybe I'll make an exception.
Thank you, Mrs. Bell. Thank you so much.

Tell your parents I said hello, Crystal.
C'mon, let's go, CJ whispers, pulling my arm out the
door. *Before she changes her mind.*

Reprieve

. . .
What?

I just got you off punishment. That deserves some
acknowledgment, don't you think?
Oh yeah, thanks for that.

That's disingenuous.
Huh?

Insincere. As in, you don't really mean it. Your gratitude is
disingenuous.
But I'm still on punishment.

But you get to skate in the contest on Friday.
Yeah, but I have to leave next Sunday.

Leave? Where are you going?
To stay with my grandparents for the whole summer.

Why?
Because my mom wants to get rid of me.

I'm sorry, Charlie.
Yeah, me too.

You're still hurting, aren't you?
What do you mean?

You don't ever really talk about your dad. I think that's probably unhealthy.
There's nothing to even talk about.

My mom says my dad doesn't talk about how he feels about stuff either. I've never seen him cry.
So what?

So, he has ulcers in his stomach.
Oh.

You can talk to me, Charlie, she says, grabbing my hand and rubbing my palm like she's somebody's mother. *Or you could write about it.*
Write about what?

How you're feeling. What's going on in your life. Like, in a diary or something.
Nah.

Scientific studies have proven that writing in a journal can keep you healthier, emotionally and physically.
I can eat broccoli if I want to be healthier.

Beethoven, Picasso, even George Lucas, the guy who made
Star Wars, had journals. It works, Charlie.
No thanks, I say, pulling my hand away fast, and
walking away faster. Woodrow Wilson's waiting.
Let's go.

I can't stand that name.
Yeah, me either.

Renaming

Woodrow Wilson sees CJ
then strolls
toward her,
burying her head
in her lap.

That's a good girl, CJ says, playing with her. *Look at those
big delicious ears. Let's play with her.*
She's blind in one eye, remember?

That's okay. She can still see in the other, right, Woodrow
Wilson? I don't think she's a Woodrow, Charlie.
It's her name, I say.

Well, now she'll have a new one.
You can't just change her name though.

We'll say it's her nickname if anyone asks, she counters.
Here, come pet her a little.
I already did.

Come do it again, please, she says, like she's my mother
and whatnot. I do it, cautiously.
Okay, there. Happy?

See, that wasn't bad. You liked that right, Harriet?
Wait, that's her nickname? Harriet?

Harriet Tubman.
The Underground Railroad lady?

She was a nurse, too. And a spy.
Like CIA?

Like Civil War spy.
You're like an encyclopedia.

Is that a compliment?
I guess.

I'm thirsty.
Me too, it's hotttt!

Eighty-nine degrees and it's gonna get even hotter.
Let's drop Wood— Harriet off and go get some sodas.

Cool.
Cool.

I'll miss you, Charlie Bell, she says, punching me in the
stomach again.

Me and CJ

walk and play
with Harriet
(well, CJ does most
of the playing)
for the next five days,
and Mrs. Wilson
even makes us
chocolate chip cookies
one day,
but while she's watching
her favorite TV show,
General Hospital,
she forgets
they're in the oven
and they burn
so she gives us
three dollars
to get some snacks
from the Quik-Mart.

On Friday

we walk around
the block
twice
'cause we know
it's our last time
and I think
Harriet knows it too,
'cause when we get
back to her porch
she sits

her ginormous butt
right between us
and sprawls herself
all over us
so we literally
can't move.

Farewell

What did you get on your report card?
Bs and Cs. What'd you get, all As?

I wish. Mrs. Toney gave me a B.
Sorry.

*The whole class got a B, 'cause Mrs. Toney believes that if
one person is being disruptive it's all of our faults.*
That sucks.

You want a Now and Later?
No thanks.

It's watermelon, your favorite.
I'm good.

Charlie Bell, you LOVE watermelon Now and Laters.
I've already had like eight today.

*Is there some law I don't know about that says you can only
eat eight Now and Laters?*
Should be. Nine's unlucky.

What are you talking about?
My dad.

. . .
. . .

Well, I guess I'll eat it then, Charlie Bell.
I gotta go. I'll see you tonight at the skating rink.

A kiss first?
A KISS? HUH?

*Harriet. Kiss her goodbye. Or at least hug her. She knows
you're leaving us.*
Yuck, I'm not kissing her, I say, rubbing her instead.
And not freaking out.

The Rink

Decked out
in our silver
Members Only jackets
and Jordache jeans,
we hit the floor.

Roll . . . Bounce . . . Skate . . . Roll

The music, pumping
the beat, thumping
we're *gliding*

        sliding

               forward

backward

Roll

    Bounce

       Skate

         Roll

Wait for it . . . Here comes
the big move . . .

The Big Move

Me and Skinny are supposed
to part
like the Red Sea
so CJ can dash through
with the jump twist
while we all bust
a REVERSE
at the same time
and the crowd goes wild
except

none of that happens
because apparently
Skinny
didn't tie
his laces
tight enough
so he trips, falls
and the only thing
he busts
is his butt
and our whole routine.

I'm sorry, guys

That trophy was ours. Dang, Skinny!
I said sorry.

*It's okay—there's another contest this summer. We'll practice
more,* CJ says, patting him on the back.
Well, let me know how it goes, I say, sitting down to
take off my skates.

What, you're quitting on us, Charlie?
No, he's going to stay with his grandparents for the summer.

Really?
Yeah.

Yo, that's the worst.
Yep.

Where do they live?
Near Washington.

That's like all the way near California.
*It's nowhere near California, Skinny. It's Washington, DC,
like four hours from here,* CJ corrects him.

Oh. So what are you gonna do up there all summer?
I don't know . . . read comics, watch TV. Probably go see
all the monuments and whatnot.

And listen to old people snore.

Probably.

Sounds real fun, Charlie.
Guys, let's focus on the positive here. It's summertime. We
can stay up late reading, go to the beach, fish, and go to the
library. Don't forget about the "I Read 100 Books" contest—

Charlie, if our best friend is a nerd, does that make us nerds
too? Skinny says, less like
a question,
more like
a sad fact,
shaking his head, and
high-fiving me,
but before I can
high-five back,
and before I can
start untying my laces,
the DJ plays
a slow rap song
by LL COOL J

and CJ pulls me
out on the floor
to skate.

Skating with CJ

You know girls and boys have different brains.
So.

Girls talk earlier than boys. We have larger vocabularies,
and we use more complex sentence structures.
. . .

Charlie, on average, girls say two to three times more words
per day than boys and even speak faster—twice as many
words per minute. The list goes on—
Great, thanks for sharing your list.

Sorry, I get nervous when I get shy and I talk a lot about
science and National Geographic *and stuff.*
You talk a lot all the time.

Not around everybody.
. . .

Have a great summer, Charlie Bell.
You too, CJ.

If I write you, will you write me back?
I don't know, maybe.

Well, bye, she says,
and kisses me

on the cheek,
and, just like that,

lets go
of my hand,

and skates away,
and my heart

almost jumps
out of my chest.

Doomsday

After I put
our suitcases
in the car
I sit
on the steps
reading
and waiting
for Mom
to ruin
my life.

Hey, Charlie!
Hey!

Conversation with Skinny

On my way to shoot some hoops, he says, bouncing
his ball.
Cool.

Which one is that?
Number forty-eight.

Any good?
I've read it before.

Must be, then.
Yeah. Galactus and Silver Surfer are about to devour
the planet.

Whoa!
Doomsday.

Yo, it's hot out here.
CJ says it's gonna be one of the hottest summers ever.

Hey, watch this, he says, trying (and failing) to spin the
ball on his forefinger.

. . .

So you're leaving?
Uh-huh.

Dag, man.
. . .

Who's gonna walk Woodrow?
Harriet.

Who's Harriet?
CJ's gonna walk her.

Cool.
Cool.

Guess what?
What?

My mom's bringing me to Washington, DC, this summer.
Really?

Yep! I'm going to Six Flags with my cousins and my aunt.
Maybe you can come.
Maybe.

Sorry you got in trouble with your mom.
. . .

Sorry about messing up in the contest, too, Charlie.

Yeah.

I'm gonna practice this summer. I'll be ready for the next contest, believe that.

That's cool!

Yeah, I'm gonna make a change this summer, Charlie.

The man—

In the mirror. Yeah, I know, Skinny, I say, laughing.

Later, he says, taking off down the street, bouncing the ball a mile a minute. *HAVE A GREAT SUMMER!*

YOU TOO! I scream back as he trips over his own feet and hits the pavement.

Steaming

It's hot
and raining.

The music
she's listening to
reminds me
of the skating rink
but it sounds
less cool
coming from
her car radio.

I look
out the window
counting
raindrops
for what must be hours
'cause we've been driving
forever.

No one says
a word.

Five minutes later
I look at my watch, and think
this is going to be an
incredibly long trip.

68 Minutes Later

Let's play some Luther Vandross.
Do we have to?

Would you rather listen to something else?
Yes, I say, wondering why Dad's music is still in the car
and why she's playing it now.

You hungry? she asks, after a long pause.
Uh-huh.

We can stop for lunch. There's a Shoney's coming up.
KFC.

I'm going to need more than one-word answers, Charlie.
K. F. C.

Okay then, Shoney's it is.
NOOO! I don't want that. Can we just go to Kentucky
Fried Chicken?

Well, that's better. We sure can. But, let's do drive-thru—
I don't want to lose time.

116 Minutes

As I pick
at my food
and count
each raindrop
that hits
my window,
she listens
to Dad's favorite song
over and over
and tries
to pretend
like she's only
sniffling,
but I know
she's crying
because sometimes
a song
can remind you
of something
you're trying
to forget.

132 Minutes

I thought you were hungry, she says.
I was.

But you didn't even finish your four-piece.
My stomach hurts. It's too hot in here.

*It's probably from all that candy. I told you about those
Now or Laters!*
It's *Now AND Laters.*

148   She turns the air
conditioning up
a little,
then turns
the radio
up
a lot
and we go back
to what
we were doing
before.

158 Minutes

Charlie, being quiet doesn't mean
we can't think of what to say.
Sometimes it means
we're trying
not to say it.
Huh?

Let's do this, she says. *I'll ask you*
a question,
then you ask me
a question,
and we'll just keep asking
each other questions
until we can get
some answers. Okay?
Don't you have to concentrate on the road?

. . .

Okay, fine, I say, but I'm not going first.

Questions

What do you call it when two chips break up?
That's not how it goes.

How does it go?
It's "What do you call it when two chips are in love?"

What do you call it when two chips fall in love?
A relation-dip, I say, trying not to smile. Can we not play this stupid game?

Where is my old Charlie, my fun Charlie, who makes me laugh till I cry? I want him back.
. . .

Are you going to at least try, Charlie?
Okay, fine! Did you love Dad?

Why would you ask a thing like that?
Then why do you just act like everything's normal?

Is that what you think?
What am I supposed to think?

Charlie, things will never be normal for me again.

Only questions, remember?

Forget about that right now. Just talk to me, Charl—

Answers

OKAY . . . It's unfair . . . It's just unfair . . . Everything
was fine at the hospital and then it wasn't, and I just
don't understand . . . We were all talking like everything
was normal . . . I was cracking jokes and whatnot, and
he was smiling, and you were gone to the bathroom, and
then he just started shaking, and he was looking at me,
but it was like he was looking through me, and it was
like he wasn't even there, and then he said something,
and I couldn't understand it, and you hadn't come
back yet, and I didn't know what to do, and then he
was breathing slow, and then he wasn't, and then when
you came back they put the breathing tube down his
throat, and his eyes were closed, and the doctors said
he had a stroke and he might wake up, and his eyes just
stayed closed . . . And then the machine just made this
long beeping noise, and just like that he was gone . . .
And I don't have a father anymore . . . And, you want a
question, well, here you go: How are you fine one day
and not the next? Why did he have to die? Where is the
funny in that? How am I supposed to be myself again?
What am I supposed to do now?

Thought

It doesn't
even feel real.

Sometimes
I find myself

looking
out my window

watching for him
to pull up

after work.
Sometimes I wear

his too-big-for-me watch
to school.

I even packed
some of my clothes

in *his* suitcase
'cause it makes me feel

like a part of him
is still here.

The worst
are

the moments
I forget

that he's gone
and then remember.

The Arrival

Two hundred and forty-six minutes later
we pull into

the gravel driveway
of my grandparents' home.

They're both sitting on the
porch just like in the picture

that hangs
on our living room wall.

My grandmother
starts speed-walking

toward us,
and before

I can barely wake up
and get out of the car,

she's at my window,
grinning and whatnot.

Lord Have Mercy

So tall and handsome like your father, she says. I smile
back, politely. *Get the bags, Percy,* she yells to my
grandfather, who's still sitting on the porch, bobbing his
head to music I can faintly hear.

The last time
I saw them (I mean her,
'cause he didn't come)
was at the funeral,
where I didn't
really say anything,
and then
when we got home
I just stayed in my room
'cause I was so sick
of everybody
asking me the same
lame question:
Are you okay, son?

Hey, Momma, my mom says, leaning over me to greet her.
*Welcome, WELCOME! Charlie Bell, if you don't get
outta this car and give your grandmother a hug,* she says,
opening the door for me.

So I do,
and I almost knock her
wig off.

Dread

Charlie can get his own bags, Mom says.
Sure can, my grandfather echoes. *Don't shirk the work,
Chuck.*

*Percy, they just drove half a day—they're tired and the boy's
hungry. Right, Charlie?*

I nod heck yeah, but
my mom,
who's now getting bear-hugged
by Granddaddy,
shoots me a look
that says, *Get the bags, Charlie.*

Hustle and grind, peace of mind, he continues, *that's my
motto. You do what I say this summer, everything's gonna
be fine. Just fine.*

I grab my suitcases
and on the walk
up the driveway
remember the things
I love and hate
about visiting
my grandparents:

Love her good food.
Hate his corny rhymes.

What
an incredibly long
and dreadful
summer
this is going to be.

Fried Chicken

My grandmother
could put KFC
out of business
with her fried chicken
that tastes like
crispy pieces
of heaven
just fell
from the sky
and landed
right on your plate
next to
the biggest slice
of jalapeño cornbread
you ever saw—so hot,
the butter
that sizzles on top
could burn
your tongue.

Yeah, her cooking
is so good,
it'll make you
want to
slap yourself.

Small Talk at Dinner

How was church this morning, Momma? Mom asks.
We didn't make it this morning. Percy's knees acting up.

My knees are made of iron. Iron Man is just fine,
Granddaddy says all grumpy-like.
I know, Percy, she says, kissing him on the head and
putting another piece of chicken on my plate.

How was school this year, Charlie?
Fine, Grandma.

Good grades?
Uh-huh.

Excited for summer?
Sure.

Food okay?
Yes, ma'am.

Your cousin Roxie is excited to see you.
Okay.

And it's like this
for the whole meal

back
and forth

them asking
me not wanting to answer

'cause I have nothing
to say

and I really don't want
to even be here.

Another piece of chicken, Charlie?
Yes, ma'am.

After

listening to Grandma talk
to Mom
about family stuff,
and my grandfather complain about
the new neighbors
who let their grass
grow too long, and
who *are probably over there
smokin' that stuff,* and

After
Mom lets me
drink grape soda,
which she never
lets me do,
but since Grandma
had already poured it
in my glass
and I'd already started
drinking it,
well . . . and

After
I've eaten five pieces
of thick, tender,

juicy meat, and
I admit, almost eating
the bone,
my grandfather belches
and says
to me:
Okay, enough playing, Chuck. Game's over. We got work
to do.

Work?

Hustle and Grind

The boy just got here, Percy. Let him relax a bit.
Hustle and grind, Alice. Freedom ain't free.

Percy, you're just talking nonsense now.
Alice, the grass won't cut itself.

Can I be excused, please?
Oh, now the boy wants to talk.

Percy!
What, Alice? He hasn't said but two words since he got here.

He doesn't have to speak right now if he doesn't want to.
Well, he's got to work.

So soon, Percy? Let him rest up.
Alice, we're about teamwork in this house. This summer, we
all got our jobs. Mine is putting food on this table. Yours
is to keep cooking that good food, run this house, and give
your sweet daddy some sugar. Now give me some sugar.

She gives him a kiss. UGH!

And Chuck Bell, you have one job to do. Just one.
To cut the grass? I ask.

To be on the team. To get in the game when the coach calls
on you. You know who the coach is?
You.

That's right, Chuck Bell, I'm the coach. Percy Bell, husband
to Alice Johnson Bell, father to LeRoy and Charmaine
and . . . your father—may he rest in peace—Joshua Bell.
Who cut the grass before I got here?

That's your response to everything your grandfather has been
saying? my mom asks, shaking her head and getting up
from the table to put the dishes away.
Listen to your grandfather, Charlie. Some of this stuff might
actually make sense, Grandma adds, smiling and patting
me on the back.

Doesn't matter about before, only after. The game isn't over
son—you gonna learn that. This is the first quarter. We're
just getting started.
Percy, this isn't the Boys and Girls Club. You're going to talk
us all crazy. Just take the boy outside and show him how to
use the lawnmower.

That's what I been trying to do, 'cause the grass won't cut
itself.
I know how to use a lawnmower, I say, then add, This
sucks, loud enough for no one to hear but me.

Thought

I'd give anything
to be at Disney World
right now.

He watches me

push the mower
shows me how
to lift the side
to get the corners,
tells me,
Proper way is to cut it at a diagonal. Looks better.
Then he keeps correcting
the way I turn
at the end
of each row,
tells me never, ever
pull it backwards.
Always push, Charlie,
to get the blades
of grass lying
in the same direction, like
little green soldiers
saluting
the sky.

A friend
of his
in a cowboy hat
and a way-too-tight
silver suit,

big glasses,
and tie
comes over
and they stand
near the ditch
at the back
of the yard
talking
and laughing,
which means
I get to finish
in peace
without
any more commands
from the general.

Conversation with Mom

How was your time with Granddaddy?
Horrible.

It wasn't that bad.
You've sent me to a child labor camp.

At least the food'll be good, she says, smiling.
Why does he have to call me Chuck? That's not my name.

Just enjoy the time with them. They're not going to be around forever.

. . .

I think I'm going to get on the road first thing in the morning.
But we just got here.

I know, but—
You can't just leave me here with them. I don't even really know them.

You'll be fine, Charlie.
It's just not fair.

I'll call you every night.

. . .

Give me a kiss. You'll be asleep when I leave.
You're not gonna marry some other man, are you?

What?
Some of my friends' parents got divorced, remarried,
and the new fathers abused the kids, and that's not cool,
so I just wanna know.

I am not getting married anytime soon, and if I did, this
new husband would never lay a hand on you, lest he find
himself pulling back a nub. You hear me, Charlie? A nub!

171

And then she starts
tickling me
and I try not to
laugh,
and then
she just stops
and stares,
wiping
her single tear,
and I try not to
cry.

I wake up

the next morning
to piano

and horns
blaring

bacon
sizzling

and sun
peeking

through
pea-green curtains.

Why are all these lights on

Granddaddy says
standing
in the hallway
when I come out
of the bathroom.

Hallway light's on. Bedroom light's on. We gonna have
problems if you waste my electricity like that, boy.
Sorry, I say.

He's wearing
a brown cap
leather jacket
and sunglasses
big as goggles
like he's about to
fly a plane.

You hungry?
Yeah, I say, wondering
if Grandma made
her famous
butter biscuits.

Good, go get your socks and shoes on.
Where are we going so early?

You'll find out when we get there.
Are we going out to eat? Didn't Grandma cook?

Too early for all these questions, son.
. . .

Don't forget to say good morning to your grandmother, then meet me on the porch.
Yeah.

174   *"Yeah" is for your friends.*
Yessir.

Break of Dawn

Apparently
every morning
before breakfast
my grandfather
walks
from his house
to a lake
at the end
of the neighborhood.

By himself.

Well, every morning
until today.

The Walk

Keep up, son.
You're going too fast.

I'm a hundred years older than you. Where's your hustle?
It's just hot out here, I say, sweating, wishing I was back
in my room with the fan on high.

It's summer, boy. Supposed to be hot.
. . .

Your mother's a real good woman. Too easy on you, though.
You a lucky boy. My mother wasn't so easy. Used to make
me get a switch from our peach tree, then we got whupped
good.
You mean "whipped."

I mean she spanked us for days, it seemed like.
Oh.

Wasn't her fault, though. She tried her best to keep us
behavin', but we were bad boys. Me and my brother. We
used to cause all kind of ruckus in that house. One time we
set a trap for a rat and caught a raccoon, then took it
to school.

. . .

*He's gone now, rest in peace. Both of us went to war. Only
one of us came back.*
Sorry.

*Don't be. He died fighting for this country. Hell of a man,
Jordan Bell. Rest in peace!*
. . .

. . .
How far are we walking?

Till the river meets the road.
I thought it was a lake.

Till I say we're done.
I'm hungry.

Faster you walk, faster you eat.
. . .

Kerplunk

When we get to
the lake
he skips rocks
on the surface
of the water
then hands me
one to throw.

It sinks.

Conversation with Granddaddy

*Dang, boy, you gotta turn it to the side, slide it, glide it,
like a Frisbee.*

. . .

You play sports?
I skate.

That's not a sport.
They have skating in the Olympics.

*Unless you're figure skating on ice, it's a hobby. Your father
played football, baseball, and basketball.*

. . .

*He was so-so. I never had time to play with him like I
wanted. Too busy working two and three jobs. But he
coulda been good.*
Oh.

*You ever have kids, Chuck, you take the time to play with
them, okay?*
Uh-huh.

Course that means you gotta know how to play something.
Yeah.

. . .

Yessir.

Okay, let's get back to the house. I gotta shower and get
ready for work.
I thought you retired.

I did. Mostly. It's a part-time job at the Boys and Girls
Club. I open the club, work for a half-day or so, help the
young folks, stay out of Alice's way. And keep her out of
mine.

. . .

180　*How about you come with me?*
Do they have an arcade?

Pinball and some other machines.
Maybe, I don't know.

Look at that! Holy bazooka!
At what?

That, he says, pointing
to the blue-gray sky
above the lake. *The sun's a coming.*
A new day, a new dollar.
Makes me wanna holler!

And then he does,
like a madman,
which makes all
the neighborhood dogs
do the same.

Breakfast

While I eat
three pieces
of crispy bacon
sandwiched between
a biscuit
the size
of a hamburger bun
with butter
dripping down
the sides,

Grandma fills
my juice glass,
wipes down
her silver-colored
General Electric stove,
and sweeps
the kitchen floor.

Grandma, um, I was thinking maybe I would go with
Granddaddy.
WELL, IF YOU'RE COMING, THEN COME ON,
Granddaddy screams from the bathroom. *WE GOTTA
PICK UP ROXIE AND BEAT THE TRAFFIC.*

I need to pack him a lunch, Percy.

ALICE, THE TRAFFIC'S NOT GONNA EASE UP
'CAUSE YOU WANNA FIX HIM A HAM SANDWICH.

Drink a lot of water today, Charlie. It's supposed to be
eighty-nine degrees.
Yes, ma'am, Grandma.

CHOP-CHOP, CHUCK!
Yessir.

My cousin Roxie

was at the funeral too,
but I didn't talk
to her, either.

The last time
I really talked to her
was at the family reunion
when we were both
in third grade.

I remember
she thought
she could dance real well
'cause all the old folks
cheered her on
during the *Soul Train* line.

She was short, shy,
kinda goofy,
and honestly
she had no rhythm
at all.

But all that's changed now,
'cause Roxie Bell

is a giant
with a crown
of braids, tall
as a sequoia,
and she walks
like there's music
in her roots.

She gets
in the truck
with a lunch bag
in one hand
and a basketball
in the other, leans
over the seat,
kisses Granddaddy,
stares at me,
punches me
in the arm,
then starts yapping
a mile a minute.

What's up with girls
always hitting boys
and whatnot.

Conversation (One-sided)

What's happening, Charlie-boy?
I heard you were coming
to the big city.

You play basketball?
HOW ABOUT THOSE LAKERS?
My father said

he'd take me
to see them
when they play

the Bullets next season
if I keep
my grades up.

You make As
or Bs?
Don't tell me you make Cs?

I know Aunt Gloria doesn't
tolerate Cs. I got straight-As
all this year. Booyah!

I'm only gonna be here
for half the summer,
then I'm going to basketball camp.

I'm playing JV next year.
Starting center, that's why
I'm going to camp, to

practice my rebounding.
You know how to rebound,
Charlie?

You always gotta be prepared
to grab the ball.
That's what Granddad says, right, Granddad?

Oh, I'm sorry, Charlie. I'm
real sorry about
what happened to your dad.

I think I liked it better
when she was shy.

She Got Game

As soon as we get to
the Boys and Girls Club,
Roxie dribbles her ball
to the gym
and starts shooting.
She doesn't stop
for hours.

My grandfather
introduces me

as his grandson Chuck
to everybody
who works there,
including the lady
who makes the hot dogs
and sweet tea,
which she pours
into a big plastic cup
for me.

He sits behind a desk
at the front door
and tells me
to go have fun,
which is not

playing Pac-Man,
since the machine is
out of order.

Instead, I head
for the gym
take a seat
in the bleachers
pull out
issue #12:
Meet the Incredible Hulk,
and pretend
like I'm not in awe
watching
Roxie silently make
every shot
before trash-talking
a bunch of stunned boys
in a game
of Around the World.

HEY, CHARLIE, COME PLAY A GAME WITH US

Roxie screams
from the court,
where she's been putting
on a show,
and of course
that's not gonna happen,
especially in these
busted kicks I'm wearing.
Plus, I'd just make a fool
of myself, 'cause
I'm no good,
so, yeah: absolutely NO WAY!

190

Four Hours Later

On the way home
Roxie tells us
that she shot
200 free throws,
150 lay-ups
75 jump shots,
and played
six pickup games, then
she falls
asleep hard,
which leaves me
and Granddaddy
and boring jazz.

Jazz

This is Miles Davis
at his best, he says,
snapping his fingers.
That's all kinda blues
under the hood.
The syncopated rhythms,
the flatted fifths,
and just you wait
till Coltrane's sax solo
starts up.
That's when the car's
gonna really take off.
VROOOMMMM!

Roxie—who wakes up
at the first
trumpet blast—and I
both say,
at the same time,

Huh?

It's a metaphor, he says

as we drive by
several big
white buildings
on either side of us.

Jazz music
is like an automobile.
That's a simile, I correct,
which makes Roxie laugh.

196

Pay attention, now,
he continues.
If jazz were a car,
Miles Davis would be

a convertible Black Mustang GT,
Coltrane would be the Corvette,
and Thelonious Monk, well, that cat
would probably be

a vintage Fiat.
Jazz is smooth.

And slick.
And it takes you places.

Where? Roxie asks, winking at me.

Anywhere you wanna go, he answers.
Granddaddy, what building is that? I ask, pointing to
my left.

Chuck, that's the Bureau of Engraving,
where they make the Alexander Hamiltons.
The what? I say.

The ten-dollar bills, says Roxie, reminding me of
know-it-all CJ.
The dollars, the cash, the money, Chuck, he continues.
But there's no jazz in money,
and no money in jazz, he says, laughing out loud.

What if you don't know where you're going? I ask.
Doesn't matter. Jazz'll take you there. Just listen to those
horns and that piano, he says, turning it up even more.
That there is some bona-fide gas-guzzling music for ya.

Mom calls

to ask how my day was and to tell me that she saw
CJ playing with Old Lady Wilson's dog. Then she says
I miss you, and asks if I miss her and I say, I guess,
and then she gets all silent and whatnot . . . So I say,
I mean, yes, Mom, I miss you, then I tell her how we
were playing Scrabble and Grandma beat us with a word
she said describes Granddaddy's attitude—*ornery*—
and, Mom, I sweat a lot at night 'cause the fan in my
room just blows hot air and it's uncomfortable . . . And
speaking of fans, Grandma was washing dishes tonight
and the kitchen fan blew her wig right off her head and
into the dishwater and she just picked it up, rinsed it
out, and slapped it back on . . . And Mom laughs so
loud and so long, it reminds me that I haven't . . . in a
while.

Saturday Morning

I tiptoe
in my socks
to the refrigerator

to get a snack.
How he hears me
all the way

from the backyard
I do not know,
but he does.

HEY, CHUCK, GET YOUR CLOTHES ON AND
COME HERE, he hollers.

Your grandmother

is out here folding clothes
and I'm fixing this shed
and if you think
we're gonna work
like the devil
while you lounge
around the house
in your PJs
reading those cartoons
and eating us
out of house
and home
you got another thing coming.

Morning, Charlie—you sleep well?
Yes, ma'am, Grandma.

He'll sleep all day if you let 'im. Teamwork, Alice!
You want something to eat, Charlie?

Stop babying him, Alice. I swear.
Can I eat first, please? I say.

Champions train, chumps complain, Chuck. Love. Work.
Eat. In that order. Time to get in the game, Chuck!

Don't work him too hard, Percy, Grandma says, walking
back inside the house, abandoning me.

No harder than you work me, baby, he says, smiling.
What do I have to do? I ask, hoping he doesn't make me
cut down a tree and whatnot.

*Love your family. Work hard. And eat well. That's all you
have to do. Everything else is a want.*
Huh?

See that apple tree over there?
Yes.

Them's my apples

he says,
pointing to
a towering tree
filled with
tiny yellow-green apples.

Ten should do the trick.
Ten? Huh?

Gotta protect 'em from disease and pests. Grab ten apples.

How?

With your hands, son.
I mean, do you have a ladder?

No, but you got legs. Put 'em to use.
You want me to jump.

Unless you're Superman and you know how to fly.

My grandfather laughs
so loud
the birds
leave

their comfortable perches
for quieter ones
next door.

Then, go over to that peach tree back there, he adds,
pointing to a smaller tree, *and pick a few of those for your
grandmother's pie. And, be careful, so they don't get bruised.
You got it, Chuck?*
I guess, yes, I got it.

Grabbing

I try jumping straight up.
That doesn't work.

I try climbing the tree.
That doesn't work.

I stand on a chair
but it sinks into the ground.

So I run and jump
and run and jump

and run
and jump

and RUNNNNNNNNN!
and JUMP

and grab apples
and snatch peaches

and wonder
how I ended up

working
on a farm.

Monday Morning

Halfway to the lake
we see Granddaddy's friend
in the cowboy hat

walking his
great big ol'
black-brown dog.

Collie Pride's his name,
Mr. Smith says, then
he and Granddaddy

start laughing
(at what, I don't know).
Collie Pride buries

his pointed face
and big ears
into me, and

I just pet him,
till he starts
barking

at a boy
on a bike
delivering newspapers.
Grandma, who joined us
for the walk, says
I think

he likes you, Charlie.
Maybe you can walk him sometime.
Sure, I say,

thinking of how
I kinda miss
Harriet Tubman.

Grandma and Granddad talk

about random stuff, like
how the trees
seem taller,

how so-and-so
ought to get
her car fixed,

and if they should
invite Uncle Ted
to the Fourth of July cookout

after the ruckus
he caused
last year.

He almost got himself
put in jail, and I don't want
these kids around

that kinda nonsense, Percy.
I hear ya, Alice.
I hear ya loud and clear, honey.

Are you excited
about going to the Club
today? she asks.

Yes, ma'am.
Then walk faster, son, Granddad snaps.
We gotta get to work.

Now put some pep
in your step.
I prefer some move

in my groove, I say, just loud enough
for her to laugh,
and him to shake his head.

Work

Roxie makes me
put my hand
in her face
while she shoots
free throws
in the gym.

She makes
twenty
out of forty,

which is pretty cool.

Then she does
the same thing
to me, and
I make
none
out of twenty,

which is not.

Escape to the Arcade

After I get
the top three
high scores
on Pac-Man,
I'm just about
to eat a Popsicle
and read
about how Ant-Man
helped the Fantastic Four
triumph over
their foes
when
Roxie dashes
out of nowhere
says she needs me
and literally
starts pulling me
off the bench
I was chilling on.

WHAT ARE YOU DOING, ROXIE?
Just come on—we need your help!

"We"?

Three-on-Three

In the middle
of a basketball game
going on
in the gym
one of the players
on Roxie's team—some boy
named Grover—was
going up
for a rebound
and got elbowed
in the face.

His nose
bled a river
so now he's in
the clinic
and she needs
a sub.

Me.

On the Spot

I told you I don't really like playing basketball, Roxie.
Of course you do. Plus, you're tall. Just stand there and
catch the ball, then pass it back.

But I can't.
"Can't" is a word for losers who are afraid to try.

Don't call me a loser.
Then try. We only need two points to win.

I just don't feel like it.
Charlie, we don't have time for this. The score is tied. First
one to eleven wins, and I am not losing to these second-rate
villains. Are you gonna help your cousin out or what?

Or what.
I'll owe you. Anything. C'mon, this is really important
to me.

. . .
Thanks, Charlie. You're the best.

I didn't say yes, Rox—
Hey, guys, this is my cousin Charlie, she says to the other

213

team before I can argue again. *He's a beast. Y'all better watch out!*

Just don't expect me to shoot, I say to her.
Oh, you don't have to worry about that, Charlie Bell.

The Score

is 9–9
when Roxie brings
the ball
up the court,
showing off,
dribbling
between her legs,
behind her back,
the whole time
talking smack
to this redhead
whose teammates
are screaming
at him
to get the ball
from her
but he can't
'cause she's like
a magician
and the ball is
her hat
and they all look
at each other
in awe
like she just pulled

a rabbit
out of it
when she fakes
a jumper
then passes
the ball
right between
Red's legs
to HERSELF
and lays up
an easy point.

Now, THAT was awesome, I think, smiling, and
wishing I could ball like that.

10—9

Red inbounds
the ball to
the boy
I'm checking
but he just dribbles
right past me
so fast
I trip
over myself
trying to keep up
and now it's three
on two
and they pass
until one of them
finger-rolls
the ball
right off the backboard
and into the net.

10–10.

Get in the Game

Sorry, I mouth to Roxie,
who shakes her head
and inbounds
to our teammate, Khalil,
a real short kid
with cheetah speed
and huge eyeballs
who everyone calls Wink.

He zooms
down the court,
zips between two defenders,
goes in for a lay-up
and it looks like
it's going in,
but wait,
outta nowhere,
Red, who apparently
can jump
as high
as a gazelle,

leaps
into the air

and blocks the shot
so hard
the ball goes
into the bleachers.
The crowd
of twenty or so kids
and adults,
including Granddaddy,
jumps to their feet
and goes wild
like they're watching
the NBA
playoffs.

We get the ball back
and Roxie calls
a huddle.

Huddle

Both of you take
your guy
to a corner,
she says
to both of us.
That'll give me
an ISO
on my guy
and—

ISO? What's an ISO? I ask.
Isolate, Cheetah Boy says, his eyes wide open, which is
ironic, 'cause his nickname is Wink. He hasn't blinked
once. *She's gonna isolate him and cross him up. Easy*
bucket!

That's all you gotta do, Charlie, Roxie says. *Just take him*
to the left corner and I'll do the rest.
Okay, I say, wiping the gobs of sweat from my forehead
after only two and a half minutes of basketball.

Awry

Wink goes
to his corner
and their guy follows him,
just like Roxie said,
so I run
to my corner, but—
Wait,

     WAIT.

          What's going on?

After Roxie checks

the ball,
the guy defending me
doesn't follow me
to the corner.
Instead,
he joins Red
and they double-team Roxie
so she can't go anywhere
and they're about to steal
the ball from her
and I'm wondering
how she's gonna
get out of
this straitjacket
and it's real quiet
in the gym
and you can almost smell
the intensity
and she's about
to get clobbered
just like in issue #11
when the Impossible Man—
and before I can finish
that thought,
my first cousin Roxie,

who knows I CAN'T PLAY basketball
who knows I DON'T LIKE basketball (anymore)
throws the ball
to ME.

Oh, I wish she hadn't done that . . .

Amen

The gym
roars like
a hyped-up choir
in church
after a sermon—you know,
like when
the pianist jumps up
and everybody
is on their feet
clapping,

EXCEPT
here
at the Club
Roxie and Wink
are the choir,
the bleachers are the pews,
and apparently
I'm the pastor,
'cause everybody's cheering
like I just saved
THE WORLD!

Hallelujah

That was, like, really awesome, Charlie! I thought you
couldn't shoot, Roxie says.
It was just lucky.

I know, but you got skills. Your release was in the pocket.
. . .

You wanna go to the court when we get home?
Yeah, maybe.

You want game, Charlie Bell, then you need a teacher.
I don't really want game.

Sure you do, she says, punching me in the arm and
strutting out the Club toward Granddaddy's car,
like we just won the championship.

On the way home

Granddaddy fills up
the gas tank
then stops
by Krispy Kreme
for celebration
doughnuts
and chocolate milk,
which is a great treat
until he starts
filling up
the car
with his gas.

Roxie tries
to laugh
but she can't
because
we're both
pinching our noses
and holding
our breath.

Practice

Before dinner
I shoot free throws
with Roxie
at the park
till the streetlights
come on,
and I miss
Mom's nightly call.

She says to call her after your shower.
Okay, Grandma.

I told her about your game-winning shot, she says, *and she
just smiled through the phone.*
*The boy makes one shot and all of a sudden he's Michael
Jeffrey Jordan.*

*Percy, maybe one day he will be. Congratulate your
grandson.*
*Yeah yeah yeah, I congratulated him when I took 'im to
Krispy Kreme.*

Those doughnuts and chocolate milk were so good, Roxie
says, and I nod in agreement.

Percy, you drank milk? Grandma asks as he walks out
into the backyard. *Now, you know you shouldn't be
having dairy—*

*Oh, I'm fine, Alice. Iron Man can handle a little milk every
now and then.*

*Charlie, honey, you and Roxie come help me open my
bedroom windows. It's going to be a long night.*

Phone Message

Grandma tells
Roxie to call
her daddy
if she's going to
stay for dinner,
and when she does
she says,
Grandma, there's a message on the answering machine.

Who's it from, Roxie?
I didn't listen to it yet.

Well, I can't get in there right now, Grandma says from
the kitchen, where she's cooking, *so go on and play it and
tell me who it is. It's probably my sister. I keep telling her I
don't check that thing.*
It's not your sister. It's a girl.

What was that, Roxie?
It's a girl calling for Charlie, she says, giggling, before I
run into Grandma's room, push her out, shut the door,
and press play on the answering machine.

Phone Message From CJ

Hello, Mr. and Mrs. Bell, you don't know me, but my name is Crystal Jean Stanley and I am a friend of your grandson Charlie. First of all, I am sorry for your loss. My mother and father let me call, as I haven't spoken to Charlie in a while and they know he's my best friend. I just wanted to say hello to him and tell him that Skinny and I miss him and that we haven't been skating because Skinny's either playing basketball or he's at Flipper McGhees, where he got a job sweeping the floor, but mostly he sneaks and plays pinball, because he says he has a special token that he can use to play any and every game in there. Well, please tell Charlie I wrote to him, and to please answer my letter before July tenth, as I will be leaving for junior inventors camp on the eleventh. Have a nice day!

Mockery

Charlie got a girlfriend
Charlie got a girlfriend
Charlie got a girlfriend, Roxie teases
all through dinner
and Scrabble
and I'm the only one
who doesn't think
it's funny
'cause even
Grandma grins
each time
she tells her
to stop
picking on me.

When we walk into

the Boys and Girls Club
the next day
the lunch lady
gives me
a plate of
hot cinnamon bites
and an extra-large cup
of sweet tea,
then claps
when I walk away.

The boy makes one shot and all of a sudden he's Kareem Abdul-Jabbar, Granddaddy says, laughing and shaking his head before grabbing one of my bites and stuffing it in his mouth.
You gonna play with us today, Charlie? Roxie asks, taking another one of my bites.

I don't know.
Then find out, Granddaddy says.

He's afraid, Roxie chimes in, giggling and pushing me.
I AM NOT!

You're afraid? Boy, when you get the chance to shoot, you
gotta launch your best shot. Full-court press your fears.
Keep it moving!
Huh?

Those are Granddaddy's instructions for better living,
Charlie, she whispers, and winks. *He's got tons of 'em.*
You don't need to explain me or my rules, Roxie. I'll say
this once, so both of y'all better pay attention and learn
something: Wanna be a gem in the gym? Be golden in life.
Wanna be a baller? BE A STAR DAY AND NIGHT,
he screams. *Got it?*

Yes, Granddaddy, we got it, we both mumble,
walking away,
more than a little embarrassed.

Coach Roxie

I decide
to play
around
with Roxie
and her friends
in the gym.

This is not play, Charlie, it's for R-E-A-L, she says,
showing me
how to pump fake,
box out,
and finger-roll.

Then we shoot
lay-ups, which
are easy
until she tells me
to use
my left hand,
which is not.

Do it twelve times, Charlie, she says. *My dad says do
anything twelve times and you'll get used to it.*

After an hour
of passing
and shooting drills,
Coach Roxie
finally takes a break
to go swimming, so I
shoot free throws
and left-handed lay-ups
till it doesn't feel weird,
then I head to
the arcade,
where I spend
half my time
over the next few days
trying to beat
a player
named JR Ewing
who beat
my Pac-Man high score
by like
fifty-five hundred points.

Scorched

Granddad, can you put the air on, please? Roxie asks.
Yeah, it's burning up back here, I say, lifting my shirt to
wipe my sweat.

Roll your window down if you're hot, he says.
If?

Boy, y'all not gonna waste my gas.
You're depriving us. We could faint, Roxie complains.

I didn't faint, and I didn't have AC for the first forty-seven
years of my life. We only had one fan when I was your age.
Wait, they had fans in the dinosaur days? I say.

That was a good one, Charlie, Roxie says, cracking up.
Here, let me play some jazz for you. That'll cool y'all off,
he says, laughing.

Good Night

Grandma gives me
an ice-cold glass
of grape soda
and tells me
that Granddaddy's knees
are aching
so there won't be
any more walking
for a while,
which, I guess,
is music
to my ears.

Friday

After finally
getting my Pac-Man high score back,
I play Roxie
one-on-one
and she beats me
by eight points,
which kinda makes me
feel not so bad,
because a few days ago
she beat me
twelve to nothing.

Saturday

Roxie comes over
to help
us clean
out the attic
and have lunch
before she goes
to shoot hoops
in the park.

You ready to go play? she asks when we're done.
Nah, I think I'm gonna hang around here for a while.

You just wanna keep your head in those comic books all
day. You need to stop looking at all those cartoons and read
something, Granddaddy says, from his favorite chair,
where I thought he was sleeping.
It is reading, I answer.

His father used to do the same thing, don't you remember?
No he didn't, Alice.

Well, then what's this I found in the attic? she says,
holding up a stack of old comic books.

My Dad's Comic Books

The Black Panther, chief
of the West African country of
Wakanda, summons
the Fantastic Four
for a hunt,
which they accept
because they need
a vacation,
but when they arrive
in one of Wakanda's
super-duper
pimped-out airships,
they get zapped
and trapped
by a vast and staggering
complex of unfathomable
electronic marvels
and discover
that they are the ones
being hunted by—WHOA—
THE BLACK PANTHER.

At 2:45 a.m.

I finish
a pack
of Now and Laters,
a can
of grape soda, and
every last one
of my dad's comic books,
and even though
I don't believe
in ghosts,
I kinda feel
close to him,
like he's here,
which freaks me out
enough
to pull the covers
over my head
and finally
go to sleep.

Three hours later

I get up
to use
the bathroom
and notice
the light on
in the kitchen
and wonder
if I forgot
to turn it off
after I snuck
the grape soda
last night.

There's music
coming from
the living room.
Granddaddy's gonna
be pissed, I think,
with all this electricity
being wasted.

When I peek
into the living room
I see
my grandparents,

sitting
on the plastic-covered couch
holding hands
staring into darkness
and listening
to the same jazz song
he plays
every morning.

Grandma, is everything okay?

Conversation with Grandma

Everything's fine, honey. Come on, let's go back to bed, she
says, getting up and hugging me out of the living room.
But what were y'all doing?

I was just keeping your grandfather company.
Why?

Because I'm his wife, Charlie.
Is he okay?

Thinking is good for the soul.
His soul? Like meditation? He does this every morning?

Most mornings. It's how he copes, how he moves forward.
Move forward from what?

Come here, son, sit down with me for a minute, she says,
rubbing my back and
sitting on the edge
of my bed, and
all of a sudden
I feel
closer than ever
to crying.

Why

He misses him too.
Who?

Your father.
Then why didn't he come to the funeral?

A parent should never have to bury their child. NEVER!
It's just the hardest thing to bear.
. . .

We all deal with loss differently. I guess he wanted to
remember your father the last time he saw him, she says,
wiping the tears from her eyes.
You okay, Grandma? I ask, fighting back the tears.

He goes in there every morning and listens to that song
because it reminds him of your father. It was his
favorite song.
How come my father never played it for me?

You and your father probably had your own songs, right?
. . .

You know it's okay to cry too. Though Lord knows, I've done enough for all of us, she says.
But why did he have to die?

There's a master plan, and I'm not the master. We just have to trust in the plan.
But it's not fair. I think about it every day. I think about the ambulance coming. I hear the siren in my dreams. I think about the doctor lying and saying everything was gonna be okay. I remember he was okay. He was sitting up in his hospital bed, and then I remember seeing his mouth drooling and the way his eyes started twitching, and I remember not being able to do anything to save him, and I hate doctors.

I know, honey. In this life, rain's gonna fall, but the sun will shine again, she says, holding
me tighter,
squeezing the tears
out of me
till they come
crashing through
like giant waves
and the sadness
and the sorrow
overflows
and I can't fight it
anymore

and I don't even want to
and my eyes flood
and my heart plunges
and I miss my father
so much.

Sometimes, I wish

I were a superhero
so I could fight back
against all the
doom
and the gloom
that's trying
to destroy
me.

I wish I could torch
all the trouble
in our world
like Johnny Storm.

I wish I could
thrash
the heartache
like Ben Grimm.

I wish I could
make the sorrow
that's in my life
invisible
like Sue Storm.

And I wish
I could stretch
my arms
like Reed Richards
all the way
to heaven
and hug my father
one more time.

Just. One. More. Time.

But for now

I'd settle
for talking

to my mother
and wishing

I could stop
seeing his face

and hearing
him laugh, and

waking up sometimes
thinking he's still here.

Yeah, for now
I'd settle for

sleeping
through the night

and dreaming
my way back

to a little piece of
normal.

Later

The smell
of fried chicken
and mashed potatoes,

the blinding light
of the midday sun
bursting

through
the pea-green curtains,
and the dribbling sound

of a basketball
wake me up
from my long nap.

Roxie, what are you doing
in my room?
Let's ball, she says, throwing the ball at me.

Practice

Today she shoots
fadeaways
and I practice
rebounding
the ones she misses,

which aren't many.

Then I practice shooting
jump shots
from the corner
and she rebounds
the ones I miss,

which are plenty.

Surprise

When we get back
from the park
I'm so sweaty
even my sweat
is sweating.

While I'm in the shower,
Granddaddy bangs
on the door
and tells me,
Stop wasting
all the water
on your bony limbs,
which I thought
was the whole purpose
of taking a shower,
but whatever.

Your Uncle LeRoy is out here waiting in that hot car.
Get a move on, son!

Roxie got all As

on her report card
so her dad's taking her
to see a basketball game
and she's invited me
to see
THE HARLEM GLOBETROTTERS,
the absolute best
and funniest basketball team
on earth.

I remember reading
a pretty funny
Globetrotters comic
and watching
a video
that Skinny got
after he went
to see them
last year.

After two weeks
at my grandparents'

I'm actually
about to have
fun.

Say Cheese

Uncle LeRoy
is my father's
older brother,
but he's shorter
and doesn't really look
like him,
except when he laughs,
which he does, loudly,
when Grandma
takes out
her Polaroid camera
and makes us pose
and while we're
all hugged up
on each other
Granddaddy lets out
the loudest fart
in the history
of farts.

SAY cheese, don't CUT it, Granddaddy! I say.

Nosebleed

It doesn't matter
to Roxie—who's got
the aisle seat—that
seats 401, 402,
and 403, our seats,
are a couple
of rows
from the very top
of the arena.

But it does to me,
because
the family
in front of us
keeps standing
and yelling
every time
a Globetrotter
dunks the ball
or does something
really cool,
which is pretty much
every play.

So, yeah, I can hardly see anything.

If watching

Roxie play ball
is like watching
a magician
at a birthday party
pull a quarter
from behind your ear,
then watching
the Harlem Globetrotters
is like watching
Harry Houdini
cut a woman in half
or reappear
from being submerged
in a ten-gallon tank
of water
with a straitjacket on.
THESE GUYS ARE AMAZING!

Halftime

Just when the emcee
comes to the middle
of the floor
and is about to announce
who will get a chance
to play C.U.R.L.Y.
(a.k.a. H.O.R.S.E.)
and possibly win
an autographed
Harlem Globetrotters ball,

his pants
get pulled down
and a basket
of confetti gets
dumped on his head
by Curly,
which sends
the whole arena
into raucous laughter.

When the announcer reads

Section four hundred,
Roxie is out
of her seat,
freaking out,
talking nonstop:
What if it's me, Dad? WHAT IF IT'S ME!

When he says,

Row W,
she starts squealing
like Michael Jackson
just kissed her
on the cheek.
Uncle LeRoy
even stands up.
The people in front of us
turn around,
frowning.

When he says,

Seat number . . .
402,

a collective gasp
fills the arena
and I can almost see
the air leave
Roxie's body
when she shrieks.

Sweet Georgia Brown

Well, look at that, Uncle LeRoy says. *You won, Charlie.*
Get on down there and give 'em the Bell business.
Really, it's me? I won? I don't know, maybe Roxie can
go inst—

Yeah, Dad, maybe I can go, Roxie repeats, all excited at
the possibility.
Now, Roxie, this is Charlie's first game. You've been to see
the Globetrotters plenty of times.

Yeah, but I've never gotten to go down on the floor like that.
It's not fair.
It's okay, Uncle LeRoy, I—

Roxie, if you want to stay at this game, you need to change
your attitude. Now tell your cousin good luck.
Good luck, she mumbles, as I stand up, making my way
down the aisle to the sound of the Globetrotters' theme
music, which sounds like one of Granddaddy's jazz songs.

Go win one for the Bells, Charlie, he says, then stands up
clapping, as does everyone around us.
Everyone except Roxie.

What are the chances?

I get up,
quietly,
inch past
her bitterness,
and make
my way
down to center court
for a chance
to win!

C.U.R.L.Y.

After he makes fun
of my haircut,
squirts me
with a fake water gun,
and throws confetti
on me,
Curly shoots
a pretty easy finger roll.

I do the same. It goes in. Whew.

He shoots
a free throw
with one hand.

I shoot a free throw.
With two hands.
It almost goes in.

He shakes his head, but the crowd still applauds me.
Loudly. Whew!

Curly dribbles
the ball
from one hand

to the other,
then between
his legs and
behind-the-back-passes
to me.

I dribble the ball
then bounce-pass it
to him.
He frowns.

He walks up
to a lady
on the sidelines,
kneels like
he's proposing marriage
or something,
and kisses her
on both hands.
The crowd goes wild.

I. Freak. Out.
But then I get an idea.
I walk over
to Curly
and kiss him.
On his bald head.

He nods, then
takes the ball,
dribbles
to the half-court line,
starts rubbing
his stomach
in a circular motion
like he's hungry,
rubs his head,
smiles,
takes off
for the hoop,
throws the ball
against the backboard,
leaps into the air,
catches it,
and slam-dunks
it so fierce
the ball bounces
back up in the air
and almost goes
in the net.

There are a few boos,
but mostly everyone
is captivated
by the dunk.

I shrug,
start walking away.
But when the crowd starts cheering,
I turn around
and see Curly
walking toward me.

He high-fives me, then
hands me
an autographed
HARLEM GLOBETROTTERS BASKETBALL.

After all the halftime excitement

I'm actually on my feet
most of the second half,
eating popcorn,
hoopin' and hollering,
but Roxie's
still quiet,
still sad,
and I feel bad,
but not bad enough
to give her
my new Curly Neal–signed
red, white, and blue
basketball,
so instead
I give her
my last lemon-lime
Now and Later,
which doesn't
make her smile
but she takes it
anyway.

On the train ride home

we thumb through
The Official Harlem Globetrotters
Souvenir Book,
reading the bios
of each of the players
and looking
at the larger-than-life
photographs.

We almost miss
our stop
'cause we're so into it
and Uncle LeRoy
dozes off.

Dad, I think this is our stop, Roxie says, nudging him.

We all jump up
and rush
off the train,
the door closing
right behind us.

We take
the escalator
up, and just
as we reach
the top,
I hear
someone call
my name
from the escalator
on the other side.

YO, CHARLIE BELL!

Going down
the escalator,
waving at me
with a single
white glove on,
and telling me
to wait
for him
to come back up
is my best friend.

Skinny in DC

What are you doing here, Skinny?
I told you I was coming to Washington, DC, Charlie Bell.

WHAT'S UP, PUNK? his cousin Ivan yells up to me
from the bottom of the escalator.
I nod at him.

What's up, Charlie?
Everything's good, Skinny. We just went to see the
Globetrotters.

They were fresh, right?
To the max.

Is that your granddad over there waiting for you?
Naw. That's my uncle.

Who's the cutie you're with? CJ's gonna be jealooouussss!
Ugh, that's my cousin, Skinny.

LET'S BOUNCE, SKINNY, Ivan yells.
I gotta go, Charlie, but we should hang out. There's a
skating rink near where I'm staying. You wanna roll?

Now? I can't.
No, not now, like another day.

How long are you here?
I think we're leaving the day after the Fourth of July.
Cool.
You'll never believe where I got a job.

At the arcade?
How'd you know?

I just guessed.
No, you didn't. CJ told you, didn't she?

Yeah. How is she?
Your lovey-dovey is fine.

She's not my lovey-dovey.
Your tenderoni.

Stop being stupid.
C'mon, Charlie, you know I know.

Know what?
So you don't mind that I kissed her?

What! You WHAT—
Gotcha, he says, laughing loud. *I'm just messing with you.*

*She's not THE LADY IN MY LIFE. Get it? That's from
Michael Jackson's alb—*

Yeah, I get it, Skinny.
Hey, Charlie, you miss home?

Yeah, kinda.
. . .

You should come to the Boys and Girls Club. I'm there
every day.
Where is it?

Downtown.
Bet!

Bet.
Hey, Charlie.

Yeah?
You know why I'm wearing this glove?

Yeah, Skinny, I know. Because you're bad.
Because I'M BAD, he sings on his way back down
the escalator.

Surprise

When I get home
sitting on my bed
next to my folded clothes
that I thank
Grandma for folding
is a paisley envelope
addressed
to *Charlie Bell*
from *Crystal Stanley.*

Dear Charlie

How are you?
I hope you're SPLENDID!
I saw your mom
and she says
she hopes you're finding
your smile
again.

I hope so too.

I'm going
to Myra Hall's birthday party,
which I know you think
is kinda strange
'cause she's always teasing
me, but it's at
the skating rink
and you know
I'm not passing that up.
I finished reading
100 books
a few days ago,
so now I'm reading
National Geographic *magazines*
in the library,

'cause you can't
check them out,
and they're costly.

I've been walking
Harriet every morning
and we're the best of friends now,
though you're still
my best friend, Charlie.

Turn over (Not good news)

Dear Charlie (cont'd)

Today, Old Lady Wilson fell
and the ambulance came,
but don't worry, Charlie—
she's okay, she didn't break anything,
just bruised her hip,
so my dad said Harriet
could stay with us tonight,
but when I brought her home
she was acting despondent,
as in glum and unhappy,
probably because
she misses Old Lady Wilson
or she misses home
or she misses you.

I miss you too, Charlie Bell.
Write me back.

Goodbye,

CJ

PS. In 1941, a Great Dane named Juliana saved a whole
family. A bomb fell on their house and she peed on it (the

bomb), which of course diffused it. She got a Blue Cross Medal for that. Random, I know, but interesting fact, right?

PPS. Did you know that PS means "postscript," as in an afterthought, as in you still have some more things to say after you finish writing. Pretty cool, right?! Have a great Fourth of July, Charlie Bell!

I read

and reread
her letter,
then fall asleep
with it
next to my pillow
and my endless smile.

Practice

I shoot
free throws,
dribble
with Roxie
at the Club,
and then
when we get home
we go to the park
to practice
some more.

I pretend
I'm Curly,
crossing the ball
from one hand
over to the other
and back again
like fifty times.

*You get a good
crossover, Charlie,
and you'll catch
your opponent
off-balance.*

Like this, Roxie, I say,
boasting
and crossing
her up,
but not fast enough,
'cause she steals
the ball
like a thief.

No, like this, she says,
crossing me so fast
I almost sprain
my ankle
trying to
get the ball back.

More Practice

We play
till the moon floats

across the sky
way past

the time
the streetlights

illuminate
the court

till my legs
are anchors

in a sea of tired
but we stay long

after playground swings
stop swinging

and the crickets
stop singing

and even then
I wanna play some more.

Pickup Game

At the Club, it's no pinball for me.
No comic books for me. I don't
even care who has the high
score on Pac-Man today.
Today, I hit the
hardwood. Play a
pickup game.
Ballin'.
SWISH!

I don't score

a lot of points
but I do cross
this one dude
over like a bridge
and I do jump
so high
to get a ball
my fingers
touch the net
and I do
catch a pass
with one hand
from Wink
and I do alley-oop Roxie
who skyrockets
to the net
with a lay-up
and we do
win.

Guess Who

Good game, champ.
Yo, what's up, Skinny!

YO YO YO!
You watched?

Dang, Charlie. I didn't know you got game.
I taught him everything he knows, Roxie interrupts, coming
up from behind. *Hi, I'm Roxie, Charlie's favorite cousin.*
Who might you be? I've never seen you around here before.

I'm Charlie's homeboy. Skinny's the name, and hoops is my
game, but love is my claim to fame.
Can you play? Roxie asks him.

Does the sun shine?
Well, today it doesn't, 'cause it's raining, so I guess not,
she says, rolling her eyes.

Your cousin's a PYT, Skinny says.
A what? Roxie snaps, with a frown.

A pretty young thing, Skinny says, laughing and trying to
high-five me, but I leave him hanging.

I know what it is, silly, but it's rude.

I was just—
Yeah, just save it. Charlie, please teach your homeboy how
to talk to girls, she says, whipping her braids, walking away.

I think she likes me. A lot.
Doubt that.

You like my kicks?
YEAH! When did you get them?

Yesterday. No more K-mart specials for me, Charlie, he
says, laughing, showing off his white-on-white stunners.
You need a pair of Jordans too.
I don't have a hundred dollars.

You're a champ, Charlie—don't look like a chump. Get
some real sneaks. My cousin got these for me. For cheap.
Your cousin? No, thanks. Ivan's gotten me into enough
trouble already, Skinny.

It's not Ivan. It's my other cousin.
Who?

Randy. He works at Foot Locker in DC.
Oh.

Whatchu doing on the Fourth of July?
Family reunion party. You want to come? I could ask my
mom and grandma.

*Nah, but you should come hang. I'll introduce you to
Randy. If your mom and Grandma will let you, I mean.*
It's not like I'm locked up or anything.

Then come to Skate Castle with me. That's where he works.
I thought you said he worked at *Foot Locker.*

He works both places.
Where's the Skate Castle?

*It's not too far. It's somewhere in DC. There's a party there
on the Fourth. We can go.*
What kind of party?

Summer Skate Jam. Six o'clock.
. . .
So, you coming?
Maybe.

C'mon, Charlie, we can ask Randy to hook you up with
some Jordans. Plus, it's the last time I'll see you all summer.
Let's get our independence. Get it?
Yeah, I get it. Maybe.

Okay, bet.
I'll see ya later, Skinny.

Envy

As he walks away
in his slick, sleek
white sneakers with
elephant print trim
and an air cushion
on the heels
(to help you jump higher)
it's like
he's floating
on air
or walking
on water
and if I had
a pair
I could probably
up my game
and do all kinds
of tricks
like Magic
and soar
like Bird.

If only.

When I get home

The man
in the cowboy hat

is walking up the driveway.
Hey, sonny, is Iron Man home?

Who?
Your Granddaddy.

Whatchu doing, Smitty? my grandfather says, coming
from around the back of the house with a hammer.
What are you trying to build now, Percy?

Always the same thing. Building a better world, Smitty.
True.

Alice wants a shed for something or another. I'm not even
sure.
How come your grandson's not helping you?

It's a good question, Smitty. These young folks don't work
like we used to.
Back in the olden days, I say, when rainbows were
black and white.

Percy, your grandson's trying to joke us.

Nice to see you, sir. Granddaddy, I'll be back, I say, rushing away before he does ask me to help him with the shed.

Conversation at Roxie's Front Door

I can't play right now, Chuck.
Why?

I'm going to the movies.
Oh.

I'd invite you to come, but it's just girls.
. . .

Here's my ball. You can take it to the court and practice.
Thanks.

*Work on your crossover and your lay-ups, Charlie. We got a
big game on Friday, and we can't afford for you to mess up.*
A big game? What do you mean?

*You saw the poster for the three-on-three Hoop Stars game
on Friday, right?*
Yeah, the Boys and Girls Club is playing the YMCA.

*Exactly, and they're our rivals. They beat us last year, and
they never stopped bragging. How do I know this? Because
I go to the same school as two of their players, and they
literally bragged about it every day at lunch, and it was*

unbearable, Chuck. I tell ya, unbearable. So, you gotta
be ready.
Be ready for what?

Be ready to play!
I'm playing?

You're exhausting.
But what about Grover?

His mom doesn't want him to get hurt again, so she said he
can't play.
Oh.

So, it's me, you, and Wink.
Oh.

Now go practice. I gotta get dressed and put on my makeup.
Wait, you wear makeup?

Bye, Charlie Bell.
Bye.

Solo

Nobody's on the court
but me,

so I play against
myself,

missing jump shots,
grabbing rebounds,

making lay-ups,
ballin' like a champ.

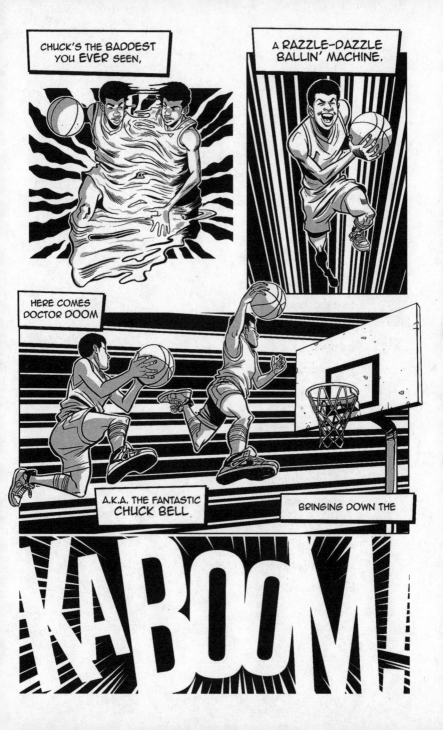

The two old men

are still sitting
on the porch
when I return
a few hours later,
their faces lit
by the fading sun,
sleeping, snoring, and
I don't want
to wake them,
so I tiptoe

up the stairs
when outta nowhere
Mr. Smitty screams
FREEZE! and points
an imaginary gun
at me
and I almost jump
outta my own skin
and then they both
sit up
and start laughing
like madmen.

You got him, Smitty, my grandfather says. *Sorry, Chuck—*
Smitty had too many hours fighting crime today.
You can't out-joke a joker, Smitty screams, slapping
his knee and laughing so hard he almost falls out of
the chair.

Say good night to your grandfather and Mr. Smith,
Grandma says, holding open the front door.

I do, then
follow her
in the door
to sanity.

Come sit down in the kitchen. I want to show you
something, she says.

She pulls out

a scrapbook
of family pictures

of people
who look familiar

but I have no memory
of.

Percival Bell, Age 22

This is your grandfather
when I first met him.
He was sharp
as a tack, cool
as a summer breeze,
serious as thunder
in his light blue polo
and matching pants,
with black belt
and air force boots.

I was at the train station
with my parents
waiting for
my grandparents
to arrive
when he got off the train
and this girl
I knew from school
come running up to him,
kissing on him
so fast,
she almost knocked
me over.

I saw him
staring at me
and I turned away quick
'cause I didn't want
him to know
I'd been staring too.

But he knew.
I think he knew,
'cause he found out
where I went to church,
which was pretty easy
'cause it was only two churches:

the Baptist
and the Methodist.

He showed up
that Sunday, tried
to talk with me, and
I ignored him.

'Cause he had a girlfriend.
Yes, because he had a girlfriend!

Tell 'im what happened next, Alice. Tell 'im, Granddaddy
says, walking in the front door.
They were always fussing and—

She fussed a lot. Get it straight, Alice.
And the next thing I know, they broke up—

Who is the other guy in the picture, Grandma? In the
uniform, walking behind Granddaddy.

Jordan Bell, Age 23

Your grandfather's brother
was a jokester,
liked to laugh a lot
and yap a lot,
especially on
the football field,
and to the girls
at church.

Your grandfather
was sweet
as apples, straight
as the pleats
on his pants,
like a gentleman should be.

But your Uncle Jordan,
he was a bona-fide mess,
always the loud one,
the life of the party.

They were both
on leave
for three weeks, and
by the time

they left
Jordan Bell knew
everybody's name
and they all knew his,
God rest his soul.

The girl
that was kissing
on Percy
at the train station—her name
was Ruth—never
spoke
to either of us
again.

And, I fell.
I fell so deep
in love
with him,
it's like I was drowning
in pure joy.
Now, that's deep, Charlie, she says, laughing
and turning the page.

Joshua Bell, Age 37

That's your father
playing catch with you
in the front yard.

He was handsome
as a Hollywood actor,
just like you.

You want a son like him, Charlie,
that's what you want.
Just a joy to—

Now, why are you lying to that boy, Alice? Granddaddy
interrupts. *Tell him the truth.*

Family History

Don't say that, Percy. Josh was a good boy.
He was a cut-up, a knucklehead going nowhere fast. No
plan, no purpose. If it weren't for the air force, he would've
been in a world of trouble.

*I seem to remember you were a bit of a cut-up back in the
day too, Percy.*
We're not talking about me right now, Alice.

*Charlie, your father was a good man, just took him a little
longer to find his way. That war straightened him out,
though.*
He told me he didn't like it.

He may not have liked it, but it made a man out of him.
That war didn't make him who he was, Charlie. Your
momma did that.

I agree with that, too, Alice.
Josh didn't stand a chance when he met her. She just looked
at him and he melted like butter. Heck, me too.

They were so cute.
Yeah, real cute, Alice. Now how about we stop all the
reminiscing.

We can all use some good remembering from time to time,
right, Percy?
I guess you right, Alice. I guess you right, Granddaddy says,
kissing her on the cheek, then rubbing my bushy head.
But after we get finished with the memories, Chuck's got to
get to work.

Work?
The grass.

But, Granddaddy, it's almost too dark to see—
Well, you better get to cutting, before you can't see.

Phone Message

Hey, Mom,
it's me, Charlie.
I just cut
the grass
at night.
I can't wait to see you
at the cookout
on Saturday,
and can you bring
my skates, please,
and some
of our records,
'cause Granddaddy plays
jazz nonstop
in the house
in the car
and it's annoying
and I can't get this one song
out of my head
and I want some
new sneakers,
Air Jordans,
PLEAAAASSSSEEE!
And do you mind
if I leave

the reunion early
and go shoot
a little hoop
just for a few hours
'cause I'm trying
to get better.
PLEAAAASSSSEEE!
And I love you.
Call me back.
Bye.

When Granddaddy hollers

Chuck, the phone's for you,
and hurry up, 'cause
I'm expecting a call
from the hardware store
about a piece
I need for the shed, I start
getting up the courage
to beg Mom
for the sneakers
I really, really,
REALLY want,
only
it's not
my mom.

Phone Call with CJ

Hello?
Charlie, is that you?

Yeah, who is this?
Is Chuck your nom de plume now?

Huh?
Your a.k.a.

I guess. My granddad calls me that.
I dig it.

CJ, what are you doing on the phone?
*Let's not waste time with rhetorical questions. What's up,
Charlie? I mean, Chuck?*

Nothing, I guess.
Well, how's the big city?

HOT!
How hot is it, Chuck?

It's so hot, I saw a chicken lay an omelet!
You're so funny, Chuck!

I'm serious. It's burning up, and they never turn on the
AC in this house.
According to the news, it's gonna be the hottest summer in
almost a hundred years.

I'm gonna beg my grandmother to turn on the air.
Good luck, Chuck. So, what kinds of things are you doing
up there?

I took the train, and I saw the White House. From
a distance. I saw where they make the money, and
Skinny's here, and I'm on a basketball team.
Wait a minute, first you change your name without telling
me, and now you're playing basketball. The world is upside
down.

I saw the Globetrotters play. And I won a basketball.
Very cool.

And I'm playing in a big three-on-three tournament.
I thought you didn't like basketball.

I didn't USED TO like it that much.
Well, that sounds splendid to me. It's good to hear you smile.

. . .

. . .

How's Old Lady Wilson doing?

*She's got a cane now, to get around, and she's still burning
cookies.*

Ha ha! What about Harriet? You still walking her?

*Sure am. But I think her other eye is getting worse.
Yesterday she wouldn't fetch the Frisbee.*

Oh.

Did you get my letter?

Yeah.

Did you like the surprise?

What surprise?

C'mon, Charlie, stop playing around.

I don't know what you're talking about.

How many letters did you get from me?

The one.

Oh. You didn't get a package?

No.

Well, I guess it's still in transit. The Post Office is so slow.

What is it?

It's a surprise.

What kinda surprise?

It's a surprise, silly. I can't tell you.

Oh.

I kinda like it.

The surprise?

Your new name.

. . .

Well, I gotta go, we're going camping for the Fourth and I gotta go pack, and then when we get back, I go to inventors camp.

Cool.

Well, it sounds like you're finding your joy again.

. . .

Good luck to you.

Good luck for what?

The big tournament. Score a point for me.

Okay. Thanks.

SMOOCHES.

smooches.

Bye, Chuck Bell!

Memory

When I was little
Mom would read me
a book each night
then tuck me in
and kiss
both cheeks
and my forehead.

My dad
would be at work
so he'd call
from his night job
and say *Sleep tight,*
don't let the bed bugs bite,
and then Mom
would say
Good night, honey. Smooches.
And Dad would blow
a kiss
through the phone
and all was good
in our world.

Tonight
I whisper
Smooches
to myself,
and almost
hear a kiss
in the air
(or maybe it's the fan),
but either way
I feel
a little more normal,
like maybe he's still here,
but not in a ghost
kind of way,
more like in a
as long as I remember him
he's still right here
in my heart
kind of way.

The Big Game

The gym is packed
with like a hundred people.

The air is filled with
the smell of hot dogs

and popcorn
coming from the cafeteria,

where we all just ate lunch.
I lace up my sneakers, double-knotting

them so I don't trip.
Roxie comes up to me

and I'm thinking
she wants to thank me

for playing on her team
but what she says,

with a real stern look,
is *Don't screw up, Chuck. Please, don't you screw up!*

Wink brings the ball

up the court
like he's Carl Lewis
running the 100.

When he gets to
the half-court line,
he passes the ball

to me, so hard
my chest almost
caves in. I pass

the ball back, then
run to set a pick
just like Roxie showed me,

which lets Wink
take off
like a jet plane

all the way
to the hoop
for a left-handed lay-up.

YEAH!

Playing by Twos

We're up 18–16
with the ball
and under two minutes left.

The guy
checking me
is talking trash
like I'm a garbage collector.

Why you dribbling so much?
Why your lips dribbling so much?

Whatchu gonna do with that rock, chump? he says,
winking at me.

So I show him
what I'm gonna do
with that rock
when I dribble
to my right
and he follows,
then I cross
like I practiced
a million times
and it works

(IT WORKED)
and he tries
to follow, but he
   slips
     slides
        and almost COLLIDES
with the hardwood
while
I go right
past him
to the hoop
for a lay-up,
and just to make sure
he knows my name
I go to slap
the backboard
(and miss)
but he's not paying attention
(Whew!)
'cause yeah, he's still
on the ground.

WHO'S. DA. CHUMP. NOW? I say.

Roxie comes over
and high-fives me.

20–16.

But wait

the ref blows
the whistle

on me?
Unsportsmanlike conduct.

They get two
free throws

and miss one.
20–17.

Down by One

I miss a jump shot.
Wink's shot gets blocked.
They hit two bank shots,
and now they're about to
cash in,

21–20.

They dribble down
the court
with a minute left
on the clock.

My guy shoots the ball
and it goes
in,
rolls right
around
the rim,
but, wait—oh, snap!—
it comes out,
and I hear
my Granddaddy
screaming
from the bleachers

Grab them apples, Chuck,
so I do,
and jump high enough
to snatch the rebound
and this time
my fingers swipe
the net.

I pass to Wink,
who takes off,
then dishes Roxie,
who behind-the-back-passes
to me,
and now it's time
for me
to get on stage
and put on a show.

Showcase

In the two and a half weeks
since I've been here,
I've missed
a thousand free throws,
clanked
a hundred brick shots,
been beat
by Roxie
eleven times,
and my game
is still dubious,
but I kinda like
playing now.

Maybe today's the day
I really showcase
my moves
and illustrate my grooves . . .
YEAH!
But wait—
why are there
two guys
checking
ME?

The Last Shot

They DOUBLE-team me
I'm in DOUBLE trouble
Trying not to DOUBLE dribble
Gotta get out the DOUBLE trap
So I *juke* one
But number two follows
So I *QUICKLY*
DOUBLE cross (*and it works*)
And he f

  a

   l

    l

     s   WHOOPS!

Hits the Splits,
I wanna shoot baaaaaaaaaaaad
But I. Don't. Know.
If. I. Can. Make. It.
If I can shake this
F E A R
Plus it's only
Seven Seconds
On the clock

And if I miss it's
CLEAR
This. Game. Is. Over.
But if I s.c.o.r.e.
We win
And I'm the HERO!
(*Don't screw it up, Charlie*)
Roxie's at the free-throw line
(*I once saw her make like fifteen in a row*)
I **shoot** her
The **ball**
And it goes over
Her head almost, but
She snatches it
  Out the air
    Plants her feet
      On the line
        TOP of the key
          No one on her
            She's **FREE**
          Ready to SHINE
            Like she's a **STAR**
              Like she was made
              For this shot
                FOR THE LAST SHOT
                And she was

And she is
And she shoots
And she

misses.

334

Game Over

When Roxie
goes to shake
their hands,
one of the boys
on the other team
starts taunting
us, then says
to her,
Maybe you should play on a girls' team.

She raises
HER fist,
ready to punch,
but I grab it,
and get
in HIS face
when Granddaddy
comes outta nowhere
and pulls me
and Roxie away.

He tries
to hug her,
but she refuses,
and I can see her

trying
to hold back
the tears.

She slinks
away, like a
wounded puppy
who can't find
her bone.

Resolve

In the car
on the way home
Granddaddy talks
our heads off,
telling Roxie
that she shoulda made
that shot,
'cause it was basically
a free throw
and there's no excuse
for missing a shot
that's free,
and I know he's right,
but right now
it sounds wrong,
'cause now Roxie's
crying more,
so I interrupt him:

Roxie, you are the best
baller I know, and it's
just one miss, but
you're gonna have
a whole lotta makes
in this life, 'cause you're just

that good, and it's okay
to be down
and upset
as long as
you're not down
and out.

She stops crying a little,
and I see Granddad
in the rearview mirror,
smiling.

Truer words never been spoken, Chuck.
Own the sadness,
don't let it own you.
That's for both of you, he says, and
I kind of feel like
he's not
just talking
about basketball.

When we drop her off
at her house
I holler
out the window,
It's okay, Roxie. We will get them next year!
And I mean it.
We will get them, I think

to myself,
'cause now
being this close
to victory
makes me hate
defeat.
I want to be
the hero
in my story.

Surprise

I take a shower
then lie down

to read *The Black Panther*
before dinner

and discover
a large padded

yellow package
on my bed.

Inside is
a picture

of CJ and
Old Lady Wilson

hugging
Harriet Tubman.

There's also
a spiral notebook

with a note
on the front:

Scientific studies show that writing a few sentences in your journal each day can be a powerful tool for successful athletes. Kareem Abdul-Jabbar even wrote a book, and didn't you say he was the best player ever, Charlie?

July 2

I run
out of the house
when I see Mom
walking down
the gravel driveway.

I don't know
if she's more shocked
because I hug her
for like five minutes
or because
I haven't cut
my hair
in like three weeks
and there's shrubbery
atop my head.

342

New Sneakers

I thought you weren't coming until tomorrow.
I thought I'd surprise you.

I got so much to tell you. Granddaddy makes me listen
to his jazz. Skinny's here with his family. I've been
getting better at basketball, but we lost the game, and
Roxie's depressed, but she's been teaching me, and I—
*Slow down, honey. That all sounds wonderful, but I have
something for you.*

What?   343
*Help me get my bags out the trunk and I just may
show you.*

Okay, c'mon.
You excited to see all your cousins on the Fourth?

Yea— Yes!
I want you to be on your best behavior.

Of course.
*And, Charlie, I don't want you accepting money from your
aunts and uncles.*

But, Mom, it's not like I ask for it. They always give us kids money. Especially Uncle Richard. I think he's rich.
He's not rich, Charlie.

MOM! It's a family tradition.
For Christmas, maybe.

I just think it'd be rude not to accept.
Well, if they offer, just be polite and say thank you, you understand?

I understand.
Here, this is for you, she says, handing me a Foot Locker bag.

WHAT'S IN IT? I say, excited.
Open it and see.

It can't be. You got my message. Thank you. Did you really? I say, wondering
if I'm finally
going to be sporting Jordans.
It just can't be, I repeat.
(It isn't.)

It's sneakers, but
NOT Air Jordans.
NOT even almost-like-Jordans.

Inside the Foot Locker bag
is a pair
of corny red low-top
PRO-Keds.

What do you think, honey? I know they're not the Michael
Jordans you wanted, but they're cute. Don't you like them?
she asks.
Thank you, Mom. I, uh, do. I do, I lie, hoping
that tomorrow
the relatives are feeling
generous
so I can get
some real sneakers. **345**

The Fourth

In the backyard
there's family
and disco music
and dancing
and burgers
and BBQ
and little cousins in diapers
and potato salad
and flies

and old aunts playing dominos
and loud talking
and love
and fried fish
and more flies
and drunk uncles handing out cash
and grape soda
and beer
and chicken
and me
and Roxie
and the promise
of a hoop
in our very near
future.

How hot is it out here?
my Uncle Richard says,
wiping his face
with the bath towel
draped around
his tank-topped chest.

It's so hot, his boyfriend responds, *I saw a coyote chasing a jackrabbit and they were both walking,* which NO ONE
laughs at.
Granddaddy hollers, *It's so hot even the Devil took the day off,* which EVERYBODY laughs at.

Basketball Rule

I ask Roxie, who's dancing with a
chicken wing in her mouth, if she's
okay, and she says, *Losing
is a part of the game.
There's always rain in
spring. Champions
dance through the
storm. I'm
good.*

Let's Ball

Roxie and I
are just going
to shoot basketball
for a little while, I say
to Mom,
who wants me
to stick around
and spend time
with my family.

I promise, I'll just
be gone
for a little while.

Okay, she says, *but be safe, Charlie, and don't be out there
too long. It's ninety-nine degrees out here.*
It's just a few hours, and we'll take breaks so we don't get
overheated, I add, and she kisses me goodbye.

The Plan

When we're blocks away
from the house
and the smell
of hot sauce
and fried fish
is faint
in the air,
and we've played
three games
of one-on-one

and she's won them all,
and we're both swimming
in a river
of perspiration,
I tell Roxie
I need
to do something.

What?
I just got to go do something.

Do something like what?
I just need to run an errand.

Run an errand. Chuck, what are you even talking about?
I'll meet you back here in two or three hours, okay?

*No, it's not okay. I'm not staying out here for three hours
by myself.*
You've stayed out here longer than that, Roxie.

But not on the Fourth. I'm going back to the reunion.
Just don't tell anyone I'm not out here.

I'm not lying for you, Chuck.
I seem to remember I was minding my business,
reading my comics, when someone pulled me away to
play a game because their teammate got hurt, and if I
remember correctly, she told me, *I'll owe you. Anything.
C'mon, this is really important to me.*

. . .

I just gotta go do something, okay?

Fine.
Thanks, Roxie.

. . .

One more thing: which train will take me to northeast
DC?

I get off the train

and the heat
punches me in the face.

I walk two blocks,
take a left,

just like Roxie told me,
and there, on the corner,

two blocks away
from Skate Castle,

is a convenience store,
a Chinese takeout,

and Soul Brothers pizzeria,
where Skinny is

standing outside
eating a slice

while his terrible cousin
Ivan

holds up
the corner

lamppost
with a bunch

of older guys
with skates

hung over
their shoulders,

drinking from
bottles

hidden in
brown paper bags.

Waiting in Line

Hey, Skinny.
Yo, you came.

Yep. I don't have my skates, though.
You got money, right?

Forty-three dollars.
WHOA! That's fresh to death. Where'd you get the loot?

My grandma and uncles.
Your family is rich.

Nah, not really.
I'ma be rich when I grow up too.

. . .
Want a slice of pizza?

I wanna skate. C'mon, let's go to the rink. I gotta be
back soon.
We gotta wait in line. They haven't opened the rink yet.

Who're those guys with Ivan?
Some guys from around the way.

Y'all want something to drink, punks? Ivan says to us,
drinking from the bottle in his paper bag.
We're good, Skinny says.

Skinny, your cousin Randy's working, right? Can he
really get me some sneakers for a discount?
Yeah, he's in there, Charlie. C'mon, let's go, Skinny says,
following Ivan, who walks away with his crew of guys.

Fight

It's hot out here. How long we gotta wait in line,
Skinny?
Stop sweating, Charlie, he says, which is
ironic, because
he's the only one sweating
like a pig.

I gotta be back home in like an hour and a half.
The line is moving, see.

356   *Hold my bag,* Ivan shouts, *and you better not put it down.*

He tosses
his backpack
to Skinny,
then runs
toward the front
of the line
with his crew,
who start chasing
this other
crew of guys
like they're about
to throw down.

Inside

Skate Castle
are security guards
with guns,
Which is weird,
Skinny says,
for a skating rink.
I agree.

The DJ plays
"I Wanna Rock with You"
and we stare
in awe
at the boys and girls
skating.
I mean, they got moves
like water,
rhythm
like waves.

Just as I'm talking
with Skinny
about how I miss CJ
we see Ivan
walk through
the front door

of the rink
drenched
in sweat
with specks
of blood
on his shirt
and a sneaker
in his hand.

And just as he's telling us
about the beatdown
they just dished out
on somebody

who was clownin' them,

and just as he's bragging
about how he
slapped some boy
so silly
the kid ran away
with just one shoe on,
someone yells
GUN!

C'MON, CHARLIE, RUN!

Skinny screams,
jetting, and forgetting
the backpack
sitting on the floor
next to us.

I pick it up
and run too.
Fast.

I make it
out of the rink
Just as I hear
a shot
and see Skinny
and Ivan
taking off
back down
the block.

I follow
behind them
past the graffiti
past the pizza shop
and I'm about

to catch up
when the strap
on Ivan's cheap backpack
breaks
and falls
and so do I.

Déjà Vu

There is one tragic sound that still jolts
me, that terrorizes my heart
and menaces me so bad
that I can't breathe. A sound
that petrifies me
and sends me in-
to total
freak-out
mode . . .

SIRENS

close in, and
I. Can't. Move.

STOP! POLICE!
Skinny looks back

like he's gonna come back
for me.

He does.
He sprints

like he's running
for the gold.

Or his life (and mine).
I see Ivan looking back,

motioning
for me

to get up,
to bring the bag,

but I can't move.
He puts a finger

to his lips,
mouths *Shhhh,*

and then
he runs. Away

from us.
Skinny tries

to help me up,
but it's too late.

The blue lights
the white noise

have closed in
on me

on us
and I have no idea

what's going on
and I can't move.

HANDS BEHIND YOUR BACK!
LISTEN TO MY COMMAND!

blue uniforms
swallow me.

Piercing sirens
scorch

my ears
and I see

real guns
pointed directly

at me
and Skinny.

The Crime

In Ivan's backpack
is a brown bag
with three sandwich bags
filled with
cannabis
a.k.a. reefer

a.k.a. pot
a.k.a. we're both getting
handcuffed
for possession
of **MARIJUANA.**

Arrested

We sit in the back
of the police car,
scared stiff—hands
cuffed behind
our backs—siren
still torturing me,
as we speed
through red lights
into the unknown.

You okay? Skinny whispers.
You knew he had those drugs? I whisper back.

Naw, I didn't know.
. . .

. . .
Why didn't you keep running?

Two amigos. That's how we roll, he whispers.
Hey, shut up back there, the cop says.

Locked Up

When we get
to the police station,
the policemen separate
me and Skinny

take us each up
the stairs
into separate
rooms with

nothing
on the walls,
a table
in the middle,

and two dirty metal chairs
with grime and
what looks like blood
caked on them.

Write your parents' phone number down, he barks,
handing me a pen and a notepad.
Do you have to call them?

*Well, either that or I can lock you up for the weekend. The
judge is gone for the night, kid, and he won't be back until
Monday morning, and since you had more than two ounces
in your possession, technically we could arrest you as an
adult, and—*
Okay, I say, scared straight, writing down my Granddaddy's
phone number before he has a chance to finish the
sentence.

You want some water?
No.

Fine with me. Stay put, he says, laughing, then
walking out
and slamming the door
on what little piece
of joy
and fun
I thought
I'd found
this summer.

Things I Think About While I'm in Jail

If I ever get out of here, I'm gonna do better
I'm gonna go out and save the world
       Carry groceries for old ladies
       Rescue cats out of trees
I'm gonna practice basketball every day
       Have the best crossover in the land
I'm gonna go to school and never skip
I'm gonna listen to all the coaches in my life
I'm gonna love my family
I'm gonna clean up my room
       Cut my Granddaddy's grass with a smile
I'm gonna write CJ back
       Listen to my mother
I'm gonna go to the cemetery.
I'm gonna visit my father.
Tell him I'm sorry.
If I ever get out of here, I'm gonna do better
I promise
I just repeat this over
and over
and close my eyes
and imagine
the Black Panther
busting through the door
to save me.

The Black Panther

does not walk through
the door, but
a man wearing a silver suit,
big glasses,
and a cowboy hat does.

My Granddaddy's friend, Mr. Smith,
walks in
with,
uh-oh,
Granddaddy.

370

Consequence (Part Three)

Thank you for calling me, Smitty.
Granddaddy, I was—

Shut. YOUR. MOUTH. Chuck. You hear me?
I nod.

Seems he and another boy were caught with the bag.
We don't think it belongs to them, but the boys aren't
talking.

Might be good for him to spend a night in jail, Smitty.
I can do that if you like, Percy, but you sure you want to
upset Alice like that?

Granddaddy, I'm sorry, I won't—
You still talking? I thought I said not to. And stop all that,
he says, *crying,* which I've been doing since this all
started. *You made your bed, now sleep in it.*

Chief, here's the paperwork, the policeman that arrested
me says, coming into the room and handing a folder to
Mr. Smith.
Yep, I think we're good here, Percy, you can take him.
Chuck, I expect more out of you, son. We all do, Mr. Smith

says to me. *You and your friend shouldn't get caught up in these streets.*

Yes, sir, I manage to say, through tears and sniffles.
Now get outta here!

So I do.
Fast.

Freedom

It takes
my grandfather
almost twenty minutes
before he speaks
a single word to me
and then he doesn't stop
except to hear my
*yessir*s every now
and then.

He exits
the highway
near the airport,
then pulls into
a viewing lot
where people
can watch
planes take off
and land.

And we just sit there.

What do you have to say for yourself?

There's a Hole in my Soul

The drugs weren't mine. I was just hanging with Skinny
and his cousin Ivan. It was Ivan's bag.
*I told you before and I'll tell you again, Chuck. This is a
team sport. You can surround yourself with people who don't
play by the rules, or you can surround yourself with those
who do. But if you choose wrong, don't start complaining
when the coach takes you out the game. You hear me?*

Yessir.
*You put the wrong people on your team and you gonna lose
every time, whether you meant to or not. You understand?*

Yes, sir.
You want to lose or you want to win, Chuck?

Win.
*Then stay in the game. Focus. I know it's been a rough year
for you. That's the worst kind of thing, to lose a father. And
a son. I wake up each morning hoping I make it through
another day without breaking down, to help me help Alice
make it without giving up.*

I just wanted some sneakers, and my dad was gonna
get them, and Mom wouldn't buy me any, and Skinny's
other cousin was gonna—

SNEAKERS? You're out here chasing trouble for some sneakers? Son, you better wise up! How you think your daddy would feel about what you done? he asks me, and just lets the question sit, lets it sit long enough for me to completely break down.

I don't mind you sitting over there crying, but you gotta say something. Now's the time.
I don't know what to say. I just, I mean, I feel, I thought everything was okay, and then it wasn't, and then I came here, and it got better, and now I'm empty again, and I'm sorry, Granddaddy.

Don't be sorry, be smart. Wasn't for Smitty, you could be headed to juvie. Or worse, they'd try you as an adult, and your whole life is uphill from there.
. . .

What's going to happen to Skinny?
What's gonna happen to you, boy? You gotta focus on righting YOUR life, 'cause you got a right to life. We're all suffering, and it's okay to feel what we feel, but we still here. We still here, Chuck.

Rebound

We lean
against the hood

of his car
watch

a few planes
land, a

few more
take off.

He puts
his arms

around
me, pulls my

sobbing head
close to him.

You know, Chuck,
he says.

You're not always gonna swish.

. . .

You gonna miss some.
Heck, you gonna miss a lot.

That's the way the real world works.
But you gotta grab the ball and

keep shooting. You understand?
Yessir.

I tell you what, though,
you'll make a lot more

than you miss if
you're not always going for

the flash
and flair.

Try using
the backboard, son.

You got me.
You got your grandmother.

You got Roxie.
You got your mother.

You got all of us,
remember that!

Okay.
Now let's get on home,

'cause your momma
and Alice

probably worried
to death.

378

I'm sorry, Granddaddy.
Yeah me too, son. Me too.

Homecoming

When I walk through
the front door
it's like
being back
at the funeral.
I can't talk.
I'm afraid.
My heartbeat
is deafening,
I don't feel any-
thing but the tears
and the arms
of my
mom.

After I hug Grandma

Mom says,
Come here, Charlie,
so, I do,
and she's crying,
and she asks if I'm okay,
and I'm not,
and I am,
and she asks
what was I thinking,
and I tell her I wasn't,
then Grandma
starts hugging me again
and says,
We are all going to figure this out together, 'cause we're a family and nothing matters more than family,
and then we all walk
into the kitchen
and she puts
a plate of leftovers
in front of me.
*I saved this drumstick
and burger for you, Charlie,* she says, and
the four of us
sit at the table
and they start talking

about all the antics
of the cookout

and no one mentions again
what I did,
almost as if they think
going through it
was enough punishment
and consequence
for me.
And when I finish,
my mom tells me
to pack.

Conversation with Mom

Why?
We're leaving tomorrow.

Why? I don't want to leave, Mom. I was finally starting to have a good time.
I have to work Monday. But maybe we can come back and visit at the end of the summer.

But I don't understand.
Grandparents shouldn't have to deal with all this kid and teenager drama. Grandparents are made for good food and jazz and fun. You should have seen your grandmother when she found out you were at the police station. She almost fainted.

Things were going pretty good until today, though. I don't want to leave. I'll be good, Mom, I promise.
I'm sorry, baby, but we have to leave.

Just when I'm starting to have a life again, you have to mess things up. It's just mean, and it's not fair.
Maybe your mean, unfair mother misses you.

. . .

Charlie, my heart's been broken too, and I thought you being here would give me time to heal. Boy, was I wrong. It was worse. I need you, son. I love you.

. . .

Everything's going to be okay, she says, and gives me the hug I guess I've been needing, 'cause it does make me feel like, for once, everything is gonna be okay.

Can we stop by KFC?
Why don't you get your stuff together and we'll see about that, she says, laughing.

I need a bag for my comics.
Just put them in the same bag you brought them in.

I have a bunch more now. I found Dad's comics.
These were your father's? she says, picking them up off the bed.

Yes.
Did your grandmother say you could take these?

I'll ask.

. . .

. . .

I miss him so much.

I know, Mom, I say, and then I give her the hug I think
she really needs.
So much. Thank you, Charlie. Thank you for this.

We're on the same team, Mom!
I know, honey.

. . .

What's this? she asks, picking up the notebook that CJ
gave me.

Oh, it's nothing, I snap, snatching it back from her.
Charlie, is that a diary?

No, it's not a diary, it's a notebook. It's private, I say,
packing it at the bottom of my suitcase.
Okay, she says, smiling, and turns to walk out the room.

Mom?
Yes, honey?

Is Skinny going to be okay?
Your grandfather says he's on his way home too.

Cool.

Now hurry up, then go on in there and give your
grandmother another kiss and tell her you love her.
Your grandfather, too. He may be Iron Man, but he was as
scared as she was.

. . .

Come on, pack up your clothes.

Mom, I was wondering?
Yes?

Would it be okay, if you, uh, stopped calling
me Charlie?
Charlie, what are you talking about?

I go by Chuck now.
You what?

I just prefer it.
Whatever, Charl— Chuck!

6:00 a.m.

I wake up
to walk
to the lake
and listen
to Granddaddy
go on and on
about random things
one last time
but he's not
in the living room
this morning
and his music
isn't playing
either
so I go
to the kitchen
to get a cookie
and I look
out the window
and see him
and my grandmother
in the backyard
picking peaches
off the ground.

Peaches and Hope

What are y'all doing back here? I ask, walking out the
back door.
We're milking cows—what does it look like we're doing?

Your grandfather and I are getting peaches, Grandma says.
Off the ground? Are they good?

*They're immature, Chuck. Weak. Scabs and stinkbugs
sucking the life out of 'em,* he says, like he's not really
talking about the peaches. *But there's a few good ones here.
There's hope.*
There's always hope, Grandma adds, winking at me.

*My back's killing me, and my knee's acting up. C'mon over
here and help us out.*
Percy, the boy is about to leave. Let him be.

*Good ol'-fashioned work ain't never hurt nobody, Alice.
Look, son,* he says to me, *aim high, reach for the sky, take
your piece of this world, and make it into something sweet.*
Yessir, I say, understanding what he's really saying. Do
y'all mind if I take my dad's comics?

Sure, Charlie. He would've wanted you to have them,
Grandma says.

And go see your cousin before you leave. She woke me up
last night trying to talk to you.

What'd she say?
I'm not your secretary, boy. Go over there and find out.

Bet

After breakfast
I go to Roxie's
to say goodbye.
I try to shake
her hand
but she hugs me
instead
then says,

I'm glad you're all right. That was stupid, though.
Yeah, I know.

Did you get in trouble?
Not yet.

*They probably think being in jail was enough of a
punishment.*
It was.

Thanks for playing this summer.
Thanks for playing with me.

And teaching you?
You didn't teach me.

I did so.

You just kinda helped. I got natural talent.

That's a lie.

Let's go play one more game, then, and see.

Don't waste my time.

Bet you I'll beat you.

Bet me what?

I don't know, ten dollars.

You don't even have ten dollars!

I do, I say, pulling out my wad of crumpled bills.

Nah, I want the ball.

What ball?

The Globetrotters ball.

I'm not giving you that.

'Cause you're scared, and you know this girl's gonna shoot your lights out.

I'm not scared.

Then let's go ball.

Bet.

One-on-One

I miss
my first jumper.

She grabs
the rebound, shoots
a bank shot
right in my face.

In your face, Chuck!

I try my double cross again
but this time slower,
and it works
just enough
for me to glide
by her
and lay up
an easy bucket.

Whoa, Roxie! You might need some makeup, 'cause
what Chuck Bell did to you
was just UGLY! I say, bopping my head.

She laughs (a little)
and we go back

and forth
like this
till the score is
eleven to nine,
and she wins
and I lose
but it's the closest
I've ever come
to beating her,
to feeling like
maybe
I'm finding
normal
again.

Keep your ball, Chuck! But gimme that ten dollars, she
says, laughing and punching me in the arm.

Goodbyes

Grandma hands me
a whole peach pie.

Alice, that's my pie, Granddaddy screams from the porch.
She shushes him.

Mom starts
our car.

Thank you, Grandma, for letting me stay here this summer.
I'm sorry about what happened.
You just be a good boy, listen to your mother, and come see
me from time to time, okay, Charlie?
Yes, ma'am.

Now go on up there and say goodbye to your grandfather.
Yes, ma'am.

Conversation with Granddadddy

*Do me a favor and listen to jazz, Chuck. It's the glue that
holds us together when we're falling apart.*
I don't know, Granddaddy. Mom doesn't like me being
exposed to a lot of sax and violins, I answer, and he
laughs so loud, he almost falls out of his chair.

You take care of yourself, son.
I will. I guess I'll see ya, Granddaddy.

I, uh, love you, Grand—
Yeah me too, Chuck. Me too. Now take this, he says,
handing me a record. *And don't give your momma too
much trouble. You're lucky to have her.*

What's this?
What's it look like?

A record.
Then that's what it is.

This is for me?
I gave it to you, didn't I? Stop asking silly questions.

Who is Horace Silver? I ask, looking at the record. Oh, wait, this is the song you play all the time, right?

. . .

Why are you giving it to me?
Why do you think?

I don't know.
I used to play it for your daddy when he was little. I want you to have it now. Promise me you'll play it.

Yeah.
"Yeah" is for your friends.

Yessir. Thank you for the album, Granddaddy. Which song is it?
The greatest jazz song ever, Chuck. "Filthy McNasty"!

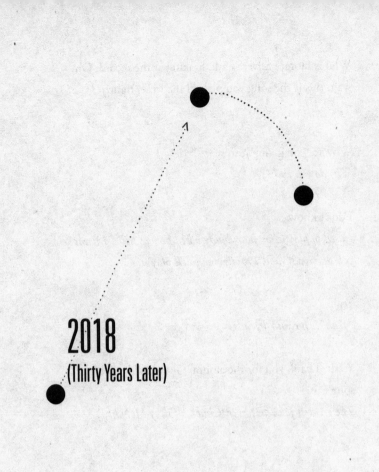

2018
(Thirty Years Later)

June 14, 2018

JB's been trying
to break
this record
for years,
but fifty free throws
in a row
is impossible,
I keep telling him,
even for the best
basketball player
in the state,
even for the number one
Tarheel recruit,
even for the son
of Chuck Bell,
but this dude
won't listen,
thinks today
is the day.

What a SUCKA!

Conversation

This is the one, Filthy, he hollers.
Yeah, I hear you talking, JB.

Who's Da Man?
Not you, fool! I'm going back inside to help Mom clean up.

Hold up—don't you want to witness history?
Nah, I'm good on the history.

But I'm doing this for us. This is probably the last time we're gonna see each other in a while.
I'll be in Colorado, not Cambodia.

I heard they don't let freshmen leave the campus for a year, though.
It's the Air Force Academy, not prison.

But we've never really been apart before.
You're always so lugubrious, man. Gimme the ball!

. . .

As in: When we leave for college, Mom's gonna be all *lugubrious* too.

Sad?

Naw, man, like REALLY, REALLY SAD.

. . .

Give me the ball!

Your playing days are over, Filthy. You're washed up,
a clam, a crab. No game, just lame.
But I can still take you to the glass, fast, and on blast.
Give it to me!

How much you wanna bet you miss it?
I'm still supersonic classy, downright in your face
McNasty. Once you floss, you never lose the cross.
And I'm still the boss.

I bet you don't make it.
How much?

Fifty dollars says you miss.
I'm not betting fifty dollars.

Dad's ring.
C'mon, son, you know I'm not giving that up. Why
would you even say that?

You afraid you're gonna miss. I knew it.
Naw, I'm just not stupid.

Okay, you miss it and I get to kiss your girlfriend.
Apparently *you* are stupid. And sexist. Geesh!

Twenty dollars, then.
Bet.

Air Ball

He turns around
tosses me the ball.

Don't hurt yourself.
Watch this, I say.

I dribble
to the top of the key

fix my eye
on the goal,

but just before the ball
leaves my hands

like a bird
up high,

Mom shouts,
JOSH, YOU AND JB COME HERE!

Graduation Gift

Your game is gone. Hand it over.
Nah, Mom messed me up when she yelled my name.
It startled me.

C'mon, bro, you're slipping. A bet's a bet.
Boys, enough of that. I have something to show you.

That wasn't cool, Mom. I was so close.
Filthy's just mad 'cause he ain't got no shot.

Please use correct grammar. Doesn't HAVE a shot.
See, even Mom knows the deal. His shot used to be
nasty, folks, but now it's just stank!

Okay, can we be serious for a second?
What's up, Mom?

This is your graduation gift.
I thought the money was our gift, I say.

This is not a gift from me.
Who's it from? I ask.

Your father.
. . .

She hands me

an old thick
padded and fading
yellow package
tied with a
big red bow.

My eyes begin
to well (JB's too)
as we inspect it,
afraid to open
the memories.

He tries to grab it
from me.

Yo, what're you doing? Chill!
Josh, it's for both of you, Mom says.

See! JB says, still trying to grab it.
I thought you said Dad gave it to me, Mom.

*He gave it to both of you. Now stop acting like you ain't
got no sense.*
DON'T have ANY sense, JB says to Mom, mocking her,
which makes all of us laugh wholeheartedly.

Okay, I'm going back into the house. When you finish this nonsense, one of you needs to walk Frederick Douglass. He hasn't been out all day, Mom says, kissing us both on the forehead and heading back inside.

I open it
and inside is
a green spiral-bound
notebook
that reads:
To: Charlie Bell
From: CJ
scribbled on the front.

Oh, snap! Let me see, Filthy.
Just hold on, I say, but he can't.

He snatches it.
Almost rips it.
And something falls out.

A letter.

Dear boys

Your mother made me
write this
just in case, she said,
which kinda freaked me out,
so I said to her,
Da Man is fine, babe.
Won't be no
in case.

When we got home
from the hospital
last night,
she was crying,
and I was holding her
trying to watch the game,
and she kept asking me
if I was okay,
and worrying
and whatnot,
so I just started writing
and we started remembering
and she stopped crying
and we started laughing.

So, yeah, if you're reading this,
then once again
I guess she's right.

This is my notebook.
It's now your graduation present.
(See, Filthy. I did write a book!)
Do not
let your mother
call it a diary!
This is my journal
from the summer
of 1988

when I was twelve years old.

When Now and Laters
cost a nickel
and *The Fantastic Four,*
a buck.

When I met
Harriet Tubman
and the Harlem Globetrotters.

When I fell in love
and didn't even know it.

It was the summer

after the coldest winter ever,
when a storm shattered
my home
into a million little pieces
and everything that mattered
became ice and ash.

When me and my skate crew
lost the big contest,
I fouled up
big-time—got caught
stealing—and not even
my mother
could save me
from almost getting
kicked out
of the game.

When there was no sun
no rainbow
no hope
and I got sent
to my grandparents.

It was the summer
I ended up in jail
and thought my life
was over.

When soaring above
the sorrow and grief
seemed impossible,
and basketball gave me
wings.

It was the summer of 1988
when my cousin Roxie
and my grandparents
taught me
how to rebound,
on and off
the court.

Later that summer

we ended up going
to Disney World
and my mom
let me taste beer
and it was disgusting
and I rode Space Mountain
so much
I literally found
my way
out of a black hole.

I spent the next
three summers
with my grandparents,
and I never lost
to Roxie again
and one summer
we played
on the same
summer team,
but the next
they made her play
on the girls' team.

After that, I saw her
maybe once a year
at the family reunion,
but she ended up
playing
college ball, and
she was pretty good
(but not as good as Da Man).

Skinny's mom
finally got their own place
when he got
to high school

(his dad got better
and moved back in too),
but it was in
the next town over,
so we played
on different teams
(he was still a ball hog
in high school, though).
He's a police officer
now, which is CRAZY!
I think you know
his daughter April
from Sunday school
and the Rec.

Granddaddy died
the week after
I graduated
from college,
and Grandma said
her heart was too heavy
with missing him,
so she was leaving too,
and she did
the next day.

They would have been
so proud of you two.
I'm so proud

of my twins,
lighting up
the world.

Shine on, Jordan.
Shine on, Josh.
Be a star.

PS. CJ and I stopped walking Harriet before ninth grade
started and it was like one day Old Lady Wilson was
there and the next day her house was for sale and we
never saw them again . . . CJ said they moved in with

her son, which was probably the case, 'cause she knew everything . . . Still does . . . In fact, years later . . . after a few high school breakups . . . after college makeups . . . after we were married . . . and living in Italy . . . she wakes me up at two o'clock one morning, craving IHOP, but since there are no IHOPs in Italy, I take her to this twenty-four-hour Italian diner called Homebaked and in between crushing a stack of pumpkin pancakes and a bowl of pickles, she says . . .

Conversation with Your Mother

Chuck, I think it's boys.
Huh?

BOYS!
What boys?

Our boys! I think we're having two boys, Chuck!
OH, REALLY. How do you know?

Because I remember doing this experiment—
What's worse than finding a worm in your apple?

C'mon, Chuck, I'm being serious.
What's worse than finding a worm in your apple?

What?
Finding half a worm. C'mon, Crystal, you know that's
funny!

*I'm talking about our children and you're telling jokes. My
experiment and many studies have shown that when a male
rat and a female rat—*
Can I finish my pancakes, please, before we start talking
rats?

I'm just saying, they're going to be boys, they're going to be
beautiful, and I just hope and pray they get my brains.

Woman, you're crazy, I told her.
And she was.
Crazy in love, you see.
And so was I.

And. So. Was. I.

Also by Kwame Alexander

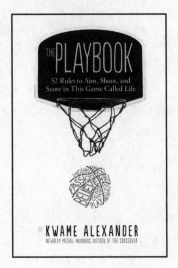

"The volume reads like a series of locker-room pep talks by a coach with stories to tell and advice to give." —*Horn Book*

"A stirring collection." —*Publishers Weekly*

"The advice never feels heavy-handed, and the author's voice shines through. . . . This will appeal to fans of Alexander's previous middle grade novels as well as young sports fans." —*Kirkus Reviews*

"Alexander uses sports as a metaphor for life in this earnest gathering of personal reminiscences." —*Booklist*

KWAME ALEXANDER's Newbery Medal—winning
novel in verse is a slam dunk!

"[A] beautifully measured novel of life and lines."
—*New York Times Book Review*

★ "Delivers a real emotional punch before the final buzzer."
—*Publishers Weekly*, starred review

Turn the page for a teaser.

Dribbling

At the top of the key, I'm
      MOVING & GROOVING,
POPping and *ROCKING*—
Why you BUMPING?
      Why you LOCKING?
Man, take this THUMPING.
Be careful though,
'cause now I'm CRUNKing
     *Criss*CROSSING
FLOSSING
flipping
and my dipping will leave you
S
  L
    I
      P
        P
          I
            N
              G   on the floor, while I
SWOOP in
to the *finish* with a *fierce finger* roll . . .
Straight in the hole:
Swooooooooooooosh.

Josh Bell

is my name.
But *Filthy McNasty* is my claim to fame.
Folks call me that
'cause my game's acclaimed,
so downright dirty, it'll put you to shame.
My hair is long, my height's tall.
See, I'm the next Kevin Durant,
LeBron, and Chris Paul.

Remember the greats,
my dad likes to gloat:
I balled with Magic and the Goat.
But tricks are for kids, I reply.
Don't need your pets
my game's so
fly.

Mom says,
Your dad's old school,
like an ol' Chevette.
You're fresh and new,
like a red Corvette.
Your game so sweet, it's a crêpes suzette.
Each time you play
it's ALLLLLLLLLLLLLLL net.

If anyone else called me
fresh and *sweet,*
I'd burn mad as a flame.
But I know she's only talking about my game.
See, when I play ball,
I'm on fire.
When I shoot,
I inspire.
The hoop's for sale,
and I'm the buyer.

How I Got My Nickname

I'm not that big on jazz music, but Dad is.
One day we were listening to a CD
of a musician named Horace Silver, and Dad says,

Josh, this cat is the real deal.
Listen to that piano, fast and free,
Just like you and JB on the court.

It's okay, I guess, Dad.
Okay? DID YOU SAY OKAY?
Boy, you better recognize

greatness when you hear it.
Horace Silver is one of the hippest.
If you shoot half as good as he jams—

Dad, no one says "hippest" anymore.
Well, they ought to, 'cause this cat
is so hip, when he sits down he's still standing, he says.

Real funny, Dad.
You know what, Josh?
What, Dad?

I'm dedicating this next song to you.
What's the next song?
Only the best song,
the funkiest song
on Silver's Paris Blues *album:*
"FILTHY
     McNASTY."

At first

I didn't like
the name
because so many kids
made fun of me
on the school bus,
at lunch, in the bathroom.
Even Mom had jokes.

It fits you perfectly, Josh, she said:
You never clean your closet, and
that bed of yours is always filled
with cookie crumbs and candy wrappers.
It's just plain nasty, son.

But, as I got older
and started getting game,
the name took on a new meaning.
And even though I wasn't into
all that jazz,
every time I'd score,
rebound,
or steal a ball,
Dad would jump up
smiling and screamin',

That's my boy out there.
Keep it funky, Filthy!

And that made me feel
real good
about my nickname.

Filthy McNasty

is a MYTHical MANchild
Of rather *dubious distinction*
Always AGITATING
                COMBINATING
and ELEVATING   his game
He   dribbles
            fakes
then   *takes*
the ROCK to the
glass, fast, and on BLAST
But watch out when he shoots
or you'll get SCHOOLed
                    FOOLed
                        UNCOOLed.
'Cause when FILTHY gets hot
He has a *SLAMMERIFIC SHOT*
It's
Dunkalicious CLASSY
Supersonic SASSY
and   D
            O
            W
            N right
                in your face
    mcNASTY

Jordan Bell

My twin brother is a baller.
The only thing he loves
more than basketball
is betting. If it's ninety degrees
outside and the sky is cloudless,
he will bet you
that it's going to rain.
It's annoying
and sometimes
funny.

Jordan insists that everyone
call him *JB.* His favorite player is
Michael Jordan, but he
doesn't want people to think
he's sweating him.
Even though he is.

Evidence: He has one pair
of Air Jordan sneakers
for every month
of the year
including Air Jordan 1 Low
Barack Obama Limited Editions,
which he never wears.

Plus he has MJ sheets, pillowcases,
slippers, socks, underwear, notebooks,
pencils, cups, hats, wristbands,
and sunglasses.

With the fifty dollars he won from a bet
he and Dad made over whether
the Krispy Kreme Hot sign was on (it wasn't)
he purchased
a Michael Jordan toothbrush
("Only used once!") on eBay.
He's right, he's not sweating him.
HE'S STALKING HIM.

On the way to the game

I'm banished to the back
seat with JB,
who only stops
playing with my locks
when I slap him
across his bald head
with my jockstrap.

MORE BOOKS FROM KWAME ALEXANDER

Spanish Edition

Graphic Novel